28 DAYS WITH A BILLIONAIRE

BENTON BROTHERS ROMANCE

KIMBERLY KREY

Candle
House
Publishing

28 Days With a Billionaire

See the other books in The Benton Brother Romance Series

Her Best Friend Fake Fiancé (Betzy's story)

Stepping In For The Billionaire Groom

❀ Created with Vellum

CHAPTER 1

Camila counted the empty dinner plates before her for the millionth time.

Thirteen. There would now be thirteen guests for Mr. Shimwah's dinner party instead of eleven. Sparks of panic flared hot beneath her cool façade.

Twelve would have been fine. Twelve would have put her exactly *one* over the expected amount of guests and—as America's finest culinary institute had drilled into her—planning for an extra guest was imperative.

But two?

She glanced through the spotless floor-to-ceiling windows and onto the scenic LA patio where Ricco Shimwah, one of the world's fastest rising fashion designers, entertained his guests. The late evening sun glistened off the ocean in shades of orange and gold, a perfect contrast to the turquoise water and white, crashing waves.

She'd give just about anything to be on the other side of that glass tonight, kicking back with a drink while the ocean breeze swept over her skin.

Normally Camila enjoyed her role as a private chef—preferred it, even. It's what she'd always dreamt of—serving her own culinary creations to LA's elite. But the pressure of the evening was taking its toll.

Two extra dishes. She groaned. *Please say Gypsy is scoring those quail eggs.*

Her phone buzzed on demand, the very sound fanning the anxious flares coursing through her. Camila shot a look at Mr. Shimwah, who was tipping his head back in laughter from the conversation. Quickly, she dashed into the walk-in pantry, pried the phone from her apron pocket, and brought it to her lips without even checking the screen; she already knew who it was.

"Did you find them?" Her heart beat wildly out of rhythm as she waited for her reply.

"Tell me again why you can't just use a freaking chicken egg like the rest of the universe?"

Now Camila was the one tipping her head back, one step closer to madness. "They cover too much of the plate," she explained in a hush. "Quail eggs are like, a third of the size, which allows the croquettes to shine since *they*'re the main event. The egg's just a compliment."

"So this is all about how it looks?" Gypsy asked. "Not how it tastes?"

"It's about both." Though, in truth, the taste didn't vary much between the two. "And if you know me and you know what I do, you also know how important presentation is."

"Yeah, yeah," Gypsy grumbled. "You eat with your eyes first."

Camilla paced before the fridge—an industrial appliance reserved for staff— hoping to ease the coil-like tightening around her throat, when suddenly a male voice caught her off guard.

"Oh, my apologies. I thought…"

She spun in place to see who'd entered the pantry of all places and set eyes on a handsome guest dressed in what had to be a tailored-just-for-him suit. Her gaze drifted up to his face. Strong, chiseled jaw, heavenly blue eyes, and a brooding, almost sad quality that hung somewhere behind his expression.

Camila gulped, a swell of tingly heat pooling around her heart.

Please say this tall spot of gorgeousness isn't Mr. Shimwah's new boyfriend. Sure, he was probably in his mid-twenties, like Camila, but the fifty-something year-old designer often dated guys half his age.

"I thought this was the restroom." He cleared his throat and pointed a thumb over one broad shoulder. "Shimwah said it'd be the first on my right beyond the kitchen."

The man's arresting gaze held hers as the moment stretched on, giving life to the sadness she'd seen there. He was rattled about something, it was clear.

"Hellooooo…" Gypsy sang into the phone.

"Just a second," she mumbled under her breath. Camila gave the guest a soft smile. "I um… yeah, it's probably the *second* one down."

The handsome man gave her a curt nod, spun right in place, and strode out. It was then Camila realized he'd called his host *Shimwah* instead of Ricco–definitely not the boyfriend. But who was he? And just what was bothering him?

"Are you there?" Gypsy whistled into the phone.

"Yeah." Camila's shoulders went limp. She would probably never have answers to those questions, and right now she had a job to do. "I'm here."

"Good. Cuz I've got your quail eggs."

It took at least two seconds to set her mind back on the issue at hand. "You got them?" she squealed.

Gypsy gave her a hard *tsk* through the line. "Of course I got them. I just...wanted to know why you needed them so bad, that's all."

Relief rushed through her limbs in a blink. "Thank heavens. And you did *not* just want to know why I needed them. You wanted to make me suffer. Admit it."

"I might be twisted," Gypsy said, "but I'm not *that* sick. I took time away from my beach meditation for you."

"Bless you for that, sweet Gypsy. I owe you big." Camila tugged open the fridge where the salad plates chilled. It was almost time to serve up the first course: bright beet ginger kraut on a gorgeous bed of mixed greens. The herb-infused vinaigrette was waiting at room temperature in the prep area, allowing for the perfect drizzle consistency. All was ready to go.

"Okay, I think I'm nearing his estate," Gypsy said. "Wow, it's *huge!*"

Camilla nodded and closed the fridge. "You haven't seen the half of it. Park on the left hand side of the gate entrance. I'll head out and meet you." It was easier than pulling Shimwah away from his guests to grant her entry.

She snuck out an exit in the back of the house, one leading to the staff's quarters, and hurried down a winding, stone-covered staircase.

"Man, this place is incredible," her friend hissed. "I'm bummed I didn't come with you on this one."

"Yeah, but if you had, you probably wouldn't have been able to save my bacon like this."

"True."

Camilla spotted her friend waiting beside the gated entrance. Platinum, shoulder length hair with a blue streak down the side, that beach wave giving life to a name that suited her so well. Carefree. Fun. Go with the flow.

Camilla's more traditional style of long brown hair with blonde highlights spoke to her personality as well. More structured, disciplined, or, as Gypsy often accused, boring.

"Royal quail eggs for your royal guests," Gypsy said as she lifted the sack toward her. "May they feast like kings."

Her sarcasm made Camilla grin. "Thank you, fair peasant. May you find fortune in the next life, as I see it escaped you in this."

Gypsy giggled. "Hey, now. We're *both* peasant girls, and don't you forget it."

Camilla steadied the paper sack with both hands, careful to slide it between the iron bars without incident, and brought her face close. Gypsy pressed her cheek in the open space, and Camilla planted a kiss there. "Now go, before the king's men find you."

Camila's list of last minute to-dos ran through her mind as she carefully weaved through the plush landscape and back to the path. She held the carton of eggs, tucked into a shallow paper bag, like a platter of champagne glasses before her, gliding up the windy outdoor stairwell with paced and precise steps. It seemed like the smart way to carry them until she reached the top of the stairs and—*slam*—crashed into something moving faster than she was.

Or some*one*.

The impact knocked her off balance, forcing Camila's weight to tip until she hovered backward over the stairs she'd just climbed.

A horrified gasp tore from her throat.

Her chest clenched tight.

And for a split second, she was forced to choose: save herself or preserve the very precious item in her hands. Her brain was too foggy to recall what that item was, she only knew she needed to protect it at all cost. A task that became impossible as a strong hand gripped hold of her arm, forcing whatever it was to tumble out of her hands and onto the red-glazed stone paving the stairs.

"Careful," the man growled. "Didn't you see the handrail?"

Camila shot a look at the grip he had on her arm, realizing it was the only thing that kept her from falling, but the man was quick to release it and take a step back. *Oh, no. It was pantry guy, wasn't it?*

She moved her gaze up his familiar looking build. A pair of black suit pants, a crisp, white-collared shirt over broad shoulders, and a black tie. Maybe it wasn't pantry guy. *He'd* been wearing a suit coat.

"You nearly fell down that entire flight of stairs," he snapped, causing her gaze to shoot to his face next. Ice blue eyes, squared jaw, and an angry furrow at his brow. *Ugh*. It *was* him.

She forced out the only word that leapt to her tongue as she remembered what lay in a heap on the ground between them.

"Eggs. The eggs. I *really* need them." She hunched down to

retrieve the goods, groaning when she realized the bag had tipped upside down during the fall. Was it possible at least one egg survived?

"Is *that* what's on my sleeve?"

Camila had heard what he'd said, but she was too busy prying open the crumpled carton to reply. Raw egg dripped from each tiny shell, answering her question with gruesome finality.

"I knew I shouldn't have removed my suit coat," he grumbled.

Camila forced her gaze off the sad remains in time to see a slimy looking yolk, bright yellow against the white, dripping over a silver cufflink where tiny diamonds spelled out the initials JB.

"You should really try and watch where you're going. I'll be stuck wearing that stuffy suit coat to cover this up for the remainder of the night."

Anger flared in her chest. "And *I'll* be stuck serving one of tonight's meals without a quail egg," she snapped back.

The man's face scrunched up. *"Quail?"* He looked like a finicky kid who'd been served a plate of broccoli minus the cheese. "Hold the disgusting quail egg on my dish, and everyone will be happy. Okay?"

A part of Camila was relieved, there was no doubt about it. But another part of her was stuck on his bossy tone. "Oh, so I'm taking orders from you now? I don't think Mr. Shimwah would appreciate that. Unless *you're* the guy he's dating…"

The man offered his hand to her, chuckling under his breath in what sounded like genuine amusement.

After a blink of hesitation she took hold of his solid wrist.

He hoisted her back to her feet with one effortless tug, but the momentum forced her to bump right into his chest.

"Nice try," he said as she took a step back. "I'm sure you know exactly who I am, which means you also know that I'm *not* dating Mr. Shimwah." He lifted those broad shoulders back into place. "I am, however, here with his top model, Adel Bordeaux."

Was *he* the second extra guest?

He gave her a curt nod. "Good luck with your meal. I look forward to it, now that it won't have a quail's egg on it." With that, he proceeded down the winding staircase, hints of his spicy aftershave lingering in the breeze.

Camila stared down at the mess in his wake. She'd assumed, after their run-in at the pantry, that he was a decent guy. Wrong. He was pompous. And rude. And most of all, *wrong* about her knowing who he was.

"For your information," she hollered over her shoulder. "I have no idea who you are."

He was out of sight now, but a low chuckled bounced off the glazed staircase. "Mmm, hmm."

Camila rolled her eyes, mumbling something she knew he wouldn't hear. "Sorry, buddy. You're not as *famous* as you'd like to think."

CHAPTER 2

*J*ames Benton checked his reflection as the makeup artist brushed powder over his face. Poker players masked their response to a winning hand, and heaven knew James had learned to do the same. It's what made most of his investments more prosperous than that of his fellow billionaire partners.

"You're on in five," called the crew manager, Bruce—a grown-up name for a young guy of nineteen who had all the ambition in the world. James liked that about him. The anxious manager repeated himself as he paced the walkway where the others sat before mirrors of their own. "On in five. Finish up and head toward the stage."

James glanced down at his suit. The slight bend of his elbow allowed his favorite cufflinks to show. He'd had to get them professionally cleaned after a mishap last month, but he was glad to have them back in his possession in time for the live broadcast.

"You're all powdered up," the makeup artist said, a hint of pride in her voice. She stood directly before him until James met her eye.

"Thank you," he said with a nod.

The brunette held his gaze and tipped her head to one side. "Hey, um…" She shot a look over her shoulder before continuing. "I know that you're dating that model, but if you're ever looking for a night out when the two of you are apart…" At once, she produced a business card from her back pocket and handed it over.

Irritated heat burned in his chest as he glanced down at the card. He and Adel weren't dating exclusively, but as far as the general public knew, they were. "I don't think Adel would like that," he said, handing the card back to her.

James didn't appreciate her assumption that he'd cheat on a woman. Beyond that, he never dated women in the service industry.

A somewhat sheepish grin formed at her lips as she tucked the card back into her pocket. "Of course," she said, attending to her makeup kit. She tucked tall brushes into a fabric case while biting her lip.

"Good luck on the show tonight," she added without looking at him. "I'm glad you're shooting another live episode. I love it when you and your siblings are all on at the same time."

The irritation he felt shifted to something deeper at her words, a scorching blade to the low corners of his chest. Not *all* of us, he wanted to say. There was one missing now.

"Let's get lined up, guys," Bruce called. "We're down to three minutes now."

James came to a stand, smoothed a hand over his suit coat, and tugged at the hint of white peeking from each sleeve.

"Looking good, little brother," Duke said as he came up behind him.

James stepped aside to let Duke and his man bun move up front; they'd announce him first since he was the firstborn, even if he *had* only beaten Zander by twelve minutes.

"Feels weird not to have Winston here," Duke said under his breath. Leave it to Duke to utter whatever was on his mind.

"Mmm, hmm," James managed. The last thing he wanted to do was revisit the loss just seconds before going on live television. As it was, he couldn't shake the recurring dream that had plagued him over the last few nights. In the horrific nightmare, James stomped up to Winston, yanked him by the suit coat, and screamed at the top of his lungs. The wording changed slightly from dream to dream, but the inquiry remained the same: *Why, man? Why did you throw your life away?*

"Welcome to The Lion's Den, everyone!"

James glanced at the nearby monitor to see what millions of others were watching in that very moment.

"I'm your host, Milo Jazz, and tonight on this special live edition, we're going to see who has what it takes to enter the Lion's Den. But first, let's bring out our billionaires, shall we?" The camera moved from Milo to the audience members as they cheered.

Duke nudged James' arm. "Some hot chicks out there tonight," he mumbled. The stage crew had learned it was best not to turn the guy's mic on until he was seated; hopefully they hadn't forgotten.

Milo continued with the introductions. "We'll start with the king of the den, the ever adventuresome Mr. Duke Benton. Give him a hand, everyone."

James blew out a pursed breath as they announced his sister next, the lovable Betzy Benton. Loveable, because she had a way with encouraging words, not because she was a pushover. She and Zander, Duke's twin, waited on the opposite side of the stage. Betzy waved to everyone as she entered, then tucked an auburn strand of hair behind one ear and gave the camera her signature wink.

James detected a hint of moisture in her eyes; perhaps she was feeling it too. The absence of their fifth and final member.

Now was the time they would've announced the youngest of the bunch, that wily Winston. If the crew had to be careful with Duke's mic before the show began, they'd had to be doubly careful with Winston's. And not just backstage, either.

Without invitation, a vision barged into James' mind: That final glimpse of Winston a moment before the casket closed. The piercing in his left brow—a tiny gold hoop—reflecting light in the darkest moment of James' life.

He clenched his eyes shut.

Stop, James. Stop. He forced his mind back to a prospect from tonight's show. One James couldn't wait to get his hands on, and rolled his shoulders back as the host announced him at last.

"You either love him or you hate him, folks, let's welcome the lady's favorite, our cunning Mr. James Benton."

James held his head high as the crowd erupted into wild applause. A sound that always pumped his heartbeat out of rhythm. His gaze shot to the leather chairs lined along the center of the stage.

Four. Not five.

The sight seemed to lasso his speeding heart and yank it to a silent stop.

He'd known this was a bad idea. Normally, they appeared in alternate episodes, one or two of the Bentons filming advance shows with fellow investors. They should've stuck to the pre-filmed stuff and left it at that. Why pretend the Benton Billionaires were "together again" when they weren't? There was one missing now, and it would never be the same.

"And now for the lion with the loudest roar, the man who puts *rude* in *shrewd*, it's Zander Benton."

The crowd cheered as Zander pulled his famous scowl and strutted onto the stage. A little known fact about the Benton twins—the two were actually identical. A detail Duke remedied by growing out his hair and, of course, behaving as his twin's complete opposite.

Once Zander stopped in front of his seat, the way James, Duke, and Betzy had, the four gave one another a nod and took their respective seats.

Milo Jazz stepped into the spotlight, brought the mic to his mouth, and fixed a serious gaze at the lens. "Million dollar companies hover in the balance tonight, on the brink of extinction. The Bentons and their billions could save those companies, but our guests will have to convince at least one of these lions to take the bait.

"Will our first owner and CEO get the help she's been dreaming of, or get her hopes for redemption crushed by the jaws of financial justice? Find out after a word from our sponsors."

James dropped his head in his hands as an ache pulsed at his left temple. There was a very good reason he and Zander had come up with the Lion's Den. Business deals such as these usually happened behind closed doors, but in their experience, many so-called desperate-to-sell prospects weren't so desperate after all. Owners who'd run their company into the ground wanted someone to save them, yet they insisted on keeping the lion's share of the company. Most hoped to borrow a few million in the dark of night and keep the public blind to their jeopardized state.

Discussing the prospects for all of America to see weeded out those trying to keep the deal under wraps and operate *business as usual.* Business as usual got them into the predicament in the first place.

"Betzy's talking to you," Duke hissed into his ear.

James blinked and pulled his hands from his face to glance at her.

She was leaning over Duke's chair, forehead scrunched up in concern. She looked like Mom when she pulled that face. "Are you okay?"

The ache in his head began to throb. "Sure."

Betzy's shoulders drooped. "I miss him too. This is weird... doing the live show without him."

"Yeah," Duke agreed. "This sucks."

James wasn't sure which was nagging at him worse—his overworked brain, his aching heart, or the tired soul within him that longed to venture out and find where Winston had gone off to. He tore his gaze off his siblings and looked out over the crowd. "It's his own fault he's not here," he growled under his breath.

"Maybe," Duke said. "Depends on how you look at it."

Well, someone was to blame, and James had blamed himself for far too long. He forced his mind back to some of the deals he'd been interested in. He'd spent hours going over the material submitted by tonight's guests. There were a few gems in the bunch, one he was particularly interested in. He only hoped his siblings hadn't seen the same hints of potential.

"You're still hosting it this year though, right?"

It. Duke didn't have to say what *it* was. Their annual celebration of Dad's life—held on his death date—had been moved to the day marking Winston's death. On the year James was supposed to host, no less.

James had no desire to throw a life celebration party for the brother who threw his life away, but he dreaded the backlash that would come if he canceled—better to become sick suddenly. Or come up with a last minute out-of-the-country business trip he couldn't avoid.

Duke nudged his arm and repeated himself, drawing out the word into two syllables. "*Right?*"

James fought back an eye roll. "Right."

The countdown started again, and soon they were back on the air. Milo introduced their first guest. James listened, watched, and nodded with feigned interest as Betzy, Zander, and Duke took turns grilling the owner/CEO about the failed state of her once wildly successful floral business, known for delivering hand-crafted stuffed animals with each bouquet. The business was leaking its profits due to one, frankly avoidable, overhead expense.

James figured Betzy would go for it. He knew what she'd do to salvage it too: toss the hand-stitched idea and wrap up each delivery with an original yet mass-produced piece instead. Keep the unique quality; toss the expense.

"James," Milo prompted, "you're awfully quiet tonight. Do you have anything to say before the lovely Mrs. Beddingfield accepts your sister's offer?"

The question made him realize that his mind had drifted. "Uh, no. Just uh…" He shot Mrs. Beddingfield a look. "Betzy knows what she's doing. You'll be in good hands."

That seemed to please the woman because suddenly she was hopping in place while stifling sobs. Nothing brought a person to their knees the way money did. Yet money hadn't stopped James from dropping to his knees over the years. It hadn't been able to save Winston, either.

He cleared his throat and forced his head back into the new contenders. A set of partners who'd gotten in over their heads with a shipping business. Zander grilled the partners enough to rattle the pair while Betzy softened the blow by pointing out their accomplishments. In the end, Duke offered to partner with them and see if they couldn't breathe life back into the project with a new business plan. He'd most likely lose money on it, but Duke was always up for a good challenge.

And then came the deal James had been waiting for. A young inheritor who'd purchased a multi-million dollar company and run it into the ground in a record eighteen months. At first glance, it was a lost cause. But that's what attracted James to it the most. His siblings would want nothing to do with it, leaving the door wide open for James to swoop in and snatch up the lion's share at a low price.

The guy stepped onto the stage after Milo announced him.

Dark, slightly messy hair, an unshaven face, and a familiar look in his eye. A look that resembled Winston to a haunting degree.

Whoa.

A hot streak of adrenaline ripped through his chest. Sweat broke out over his palms. Slowly, eyes pasted on the twenty-year-old kid, James drew in a steady breath, hoping to quell the chaos erupting beneath the surface. But all he could see was Winston and his bruised arms and uncontrollable ticks. The messy state of his penthouse. The ruined state of his life.

"Tell us about yourself," Milo said as he shook the guy's hand.

"My name is Peter Shultz, and I bought the multi-million dollar studio company called Snap Photography." He ran a hand up the back of his neck and twitched. A twitch James would recognize anywhere.

Peter. Peter Shultz. Already James could see the name etched into a cold marble tombstone like Winston's. He was on the same path; it was easy to see.

"I outspent our profits," the kid added, "which put the company into bankruptcy—"

"Why?" James snapped, locking eyes with the young guest.

The kid twitched again, then rubbed his nose with the back of his hand. "I'm sorry, sir, what was that?" he asked.

Somewhere in the back of James' mind, he knew this wasn't his brother. But that fact was a distant blur compared to the telltale tics and dark, desperate eyes.

"I asked you *why?*" James shot to his feet, his recurring dream coming to life like a raging storm. Before he could stop himself, he bolted toward him until they were face to face.

"Why did you run your life into the ground?" The storm raged

17

on, and before James could stop it, he was reaching out, fisting the guest's sweater in both hands. His pulse was loud, his crazed mind even louder, but still he heard the gasps from the crowd.

"Whoa, dude," Duke mumbled under his breath.

"James?" Betzy hissed, alarm tightening her voice.

From the corner of his eye, James saw Zander shoot to his feet. But James wanted his reply.

"I...um." The kid managed a shrug and sniffed. "You mean the business? I guess because I didn't know how to run a company."

Didn't know how to run the company, or didn't know how to break his habit? "Then you find someone who *does*," James snapped. "You get *help!*"

Peter gave a pleading look to Milo, his forehead beading with sweat, then set his gaze back on James and shrugged once again. "That's why I'm here."

The security crew hurried onto the scene, two men dressed in black standing at either side of the action. It took James a moment to realize *he* was the center of that action.

He looked down at his grip, the knotted sweater bulging from each tightened fist, as the horrible realization sank in— he'd just freaked out on a guest on live TV.

Reality struck him like a cold blow to the back. One that might rob his next breath. Gulping, James forced his fingers to uncurl and release the grip. "You're too late," he mumbled. "Your company's already dead."

Another round of gasps sounded throughout the crowd in staggered bursts.

"So what you're saying, James," Milo said, attempting to

lighten things with a chuckle, "is that *you're* not interested in this particular—"

"That's not what I'm saying," James assured with the shake of his head. How many times had Winston rejected their pleas to accept treatment? Or accepted, only to walk out after hitting that three-days-clean mark? How many times had James, Zander, Betzy, and Duke loaned him money he'd only thrown away?

"I'm speaking for me and *all* of the Bentons when I say that *none* of us are interested in this corpse of a company. You're wasting your time a*nd* ours." He shot a look to Milo next. "Get him out of here. *Now*."

Chatter broke out over the crowd anew.

"Thank you for coming to the Lion's Den, Mr. Shultz," Milo said, his even tone clashing with the shock on his face. "If you wouldn't mind following my friend Bruce backstage, he'll see to it that you're taken care of."

James glanced over to Betzy, who pressed a hand against her chest. She shook her head, looking at James the way she must've looked at Winston when he was out of control. Duke looked more amused than anything, a wry smile tugging at one side of his lips while he looked over the crowd.

Hesitantly, James let his gaze dart to Zander, who was lowering himself back into his seat. His older brother shot him a burning glare of reprove.

James exhaled a jagged breath as a pounding pulsed in his head. Zander planned to lecture him after the show for sure, but James wouldn't stick around to hear it. He smoothed a sweaty palm over his suit coat, spun to give Milo and the audience a nod, and set his eyes on the break in the backstage curtain.

This wasn't going to look good, especially after the scandal of Winston's overdose. As if the private plane crash hadn't been enough five years back—the one that took both Dad and Grandpa Benton to an early grave.

The family was hoping to dispel rumors that they were falling apart. But how could they do that when James *was* falling apart? And he was sick of pretending he'd somehow healed over the last year. He hadn't. Beneath the sliver thin scab of distraction, the wound had dug itself deeper with each passing week. No multi-million dollar deal or fancy dinner party would help. Somehow, James needed to move on from the loss before it ate him alive.

With that thought, James strode toward the break in the curtain—his escape from the shattered façade—and stormed out of the studio and through the back exit where his car waited.

His driver, Leonard, hurried out of the car, a stunned expression on his face.

"Done so soon, Mr. Benton?"

James put a hand up to stay him. "I can get the door. Head to the penthouse, please."

"James, wait!" Duke's voice came from behind.

James clenched his fists. "I don't want to talk about it," he growled, spinning back to face him.

"Then don't," Duke said. "I just…wanted to see where you're going."

"Away." The adrenaline coursing through him felt clogged

suddenly. He shifted his weight from one foot to the next; if he didn't keep moving he'd explode.

His brother's inquiring gaze took in more than James wanted to give him.

Duke knew.

Knew how hard this was. Winston might have been closest to James, especially during their youth, but Duke always had more in common with him. The two had become very close over the years.

James cupped his jaw as it threatened to tremble, the pain becoming too much to bear. Eyes misting with tears, he searched Duke's face, a sudden desperation gripping hold of him.

"How'd you do it, Duke?" he finally asked. "How the hell are you still breathing?"

Duke smeared a hand over his face and looked away with a sniff. "Dude, I just changed my life for a while. Started doing every-thing different. Like, the opposite of what I did before he died. For me, that was taking fewer risks. Dating less chicks," he said with a laugh. "Becoming more…intentional about my decisions. So I basically turned into boring old Zander." He shrugged, then set his gaze back on James. "For you, I guess it'd be taking *more* chances. Maybe…taking off without tying up every loose end at work. Try dating a woman who's *not* in the million-dollar range for once."

None of that sounded appealing, but James knew it was time to try something new. He felt like living proof of Einstein's definition of insanity: doing the same thing while expecting different results. Perhaps Duke was right; it was time to do something different. Drastic, even. But what?

"Why don't you take off? Don't tell anyone where you're going. Go to Venice. Asia. Heck, San Francisco. Just go, and don't tell anyone where you are."

James shook his head. "I can't."

"Sure you can. How many people do you pay to keep things running like clockwork? Stephanie is like...*You Number Two*. She can do anything you can do. Probably better."

James chuckled at the mention of his personal assistant. Stephanie was pretty great.

"I'll think about it." He already was, in truth. But none of the places that came to mind held any appeal. Most of his favored vacation spots had memories of Winston attached to them. Some because they'd vacationed together, like the place in Greece. Or others, because James' getaway had been dampened by a worried call over Winston and his troubled ways.

"Hey," Duke blurted, grabbing his arm. "I've got the perfect place. Vanessa and I were supposed to spend a few weeks on the east coast, but she can't go now. I've got a place on the beach for the entire month starting yesterday."

James lifted a brow. "And no one else knows about it?"

"No one. The resort has a strict privacy policy too. It's said that what happens at the Royal Palm, *stays* at the Royal Palm."

Duke's idea held a surprising appeal, one he couldn't put his finger on.

A recollection of Winston's journal came to mind, an item James had been neglecting since his death. Perhaps it was time to do something he'd been dreading for an entire year.

"I gotta get back in there before big bad Zander comes looking for us. Just get out a town for a while." Duke darted a look over his shoulder. "The place is all yours. Go there. Now, in fact. Do whatever it is you *wouldn't* normally do. The crazier the better. I'll cover for you with Zander and Betz."

At last, James nodded.

"Good," Duke said, his chest puffing with air. "I want a full report once the month's through."

James already knew that "full report" wouldn't contain the sort of details his wild older brother hoped it would. No romantic rendezvous, no parties at the local club or late-night strolls along the moonlit beach. There was something different on the agenda, but hopefully it would start the healing process at last. "Thanks, man. I'm going to get out of here."

Duke pulled his phone from his pocket. "I'll send you the specifics now. I really think you're going to thank me for this."

James hoped so.

Once he was settled into the backseat, James pulled out his own phone, a fresh determination urging him forward. He tapped the corner of his screen to dial his personal assistant, Stephanie Rell. No doubt she'd been watching the show; James was surprised the woman hadn't called him the moment he'd stomped off the live taping.

The ringing stopped a half second before she spoke up.

"What in the freaking world got into you, James Benton?"

That was the reaction he'd expected. "I'm heading out of town and I need you to cover for me."

Stunned silence fell over the line. "James…"

"*Please.*" He hoped that would put a stop to her prying. Stephanie was, as Duke said, like a second version of James. But the truth was, he'd been sensing a change in her over the last few weeks. A change that had her looking at him longer, talking in sweeter tones, and prying more than she ever had before. He

needed to make sure the lines were still drawn clearly, especially in moments like these.

"Of course," she said in a whisper. "When do you leave?"

James pictured the chopper at his estate, and the short trip
to the runway where his jet waited nearby. When would he be
leaving? The answer to that was clear. "Within the hour."

CHAPTER 3

*C*amila sighed as she looked over the limited view from her apartment patio. If she looked beyond the neighboring cafes, bars, and office buildings, she could spot a distant view of the beach. Turquoise water, white, rolling waves, and swaying palms. Her immediate view wasn't quite so serene. An endless array of vehicles switching lanes, pausing at intersections, and managing to parallel park along Main Street.

A deep sigh escaped her lips. It had been a rough month. Her once-growing list of elites in the fashion industry had dwindled, along with the referrals she might have gained from them. All because of one slip-up at Shimwah's dinner party.

"She's got a new one," Gypsy said as she plopped into Camila's hammock with the phone in her hand. Sunlight spilled over the porch, causing her to squint as she read. "Wait, let me summon her whiney little voice." She cleared her throat and scrunched up her nose. "Grossest food ever at Lauren Clide's last night. Guys, if you want the name of my private chef, just ask. Please. For the love."

Angry heat flared in Camila's blood as she considered the damage such posts could do. After Camila's run-in with the brooding jerk on the stairs, the famous model posted about the *"clumsy cook who spilled raw egg"* all over her date. She'd mentioned her by name, tagging Camila's catering page. Adel had even encouraged fans to reenact the mishap while she reposted her favorites.

Humiliation gripped Camila each time she recalled one of the ridiculous skits. Sloppy-looking cooks in chef hats and kitchen whites. Most carried a dozen chicken eggs, not the tiny quail eggs that had been at the scene. Some portrayals featured several dozen eggs crashing over the "victim".

If it hadn't been so damaging to both her ego and her career, Camila might have laughed at the video clips. As it was, the entourage had sent her into hiding. One she promised herself would be temporary.

"Why does anyone even listen to that woman where food is concerned? She glares at a lens for a living."

Gypsy shrugged. "Who knows. I still think you should speak out about it. This is cyber bullying. By some famous chick that people look up to, no less."

Camila did her best to avoid the scrutinizing look she knew her friend was casting her way.

"It just doesn't seem like you," Gypsy persisted. "You're not the lay-down-and-take-it type."

A cold chill rumbled beneath her skin. Camila rubbed a hand over her arm, willing the dark incident from her past to stay right where it belonged—the past. The truth was, if Camila made an even bigger spectacle of herself by challenging the woman head-on, Adel might dig deeper. Expose parts of her past that no one had the right to know. A part she hadn't even told Gypsy about.

"At least she's not just bashing *you*," Gypsy finally said. "Pretty soon she'll have her little followers slamming someone else with their lame reenactments." She sneered at the phone screen. "What *I* want to know, is why anyone would invite her to their dinner party. All she does is complain about them."

Camila forced her mind to shift as she eyed the distant palm trees swaying against the sunrise. She'd done her best to live with her face to the sun, to soak up the warmth this life had to offer. But having her name out there summoned that all-too-familiar fear. Had her wanting to hide in the shadows once more.

She glanced over at Gypsy, who was mumbling something under her breath. "Are people *that* desperate to have their name attached to her right now? Who cares if she's bashing the chef or the DJ? Adel Bordeaux actually showed up at *my* party." She spun a circle in the air with her finger and rolled her eyes.

Camila couldn't help but smile. Her friend had a way of calming her fears without even being aware of it. She was good for her that way.

"Holy crap!" Gypsy blurted, her finger on the phone as she scrolled. She climbed out of the hammock in a rush, leaving the thing to wobble and sway behind her. "Adel's boyfriend—the guy you bumped into—is *losing* it!"

Camila set her mug down in time to steady the phone Gypsy held in front of her. She recognized the man easily enough now that she knew who he was.

Her heart pumped a few hot beats out of rhythm as the camera zoomed into a shot filmed on the Benton's TV show. James Benton jumped up from his leather chair and snatched some guy—looked like he was a guest—by the front of his shirt. The camera caught shots of Mr. Benton's clenched jaw, flared nostrils, and angry deep blue eyes.

Camila leaned toward the phone to hear him better, which proved unnecessary since he was yelling.

"...none of us are interested in this corpse of a company. You're wasting your time and ours. Get him out of here," he spat. *"Now!"*

Camila gasped in surprise. Despite the man's unsavory manner at the dinner party, she hadn't thought he was as cruel as the company he kept. Perhaps he was. Thank heavens he hadn't spread his venom her way. Adel had done enough damage on her own.

But then Camila noticed something in the clip: the brief glances exchanged between his siblings after the fact. Filled with shock and concern. And James—he looked...distraught.

A small knot of pain pricked her heart. She'd seen that kind of hurt before. Had experienced it herself, even. Perhaps this was out of character for him.

Gypsy tapped the screen as it came to an end. "Looks like his nasty little girlfriend is rubbing off on him. That couple is pure evil." She wiggled her fingers while repeating the word in a slow trill. *"Eeeevil..."*

Camila managed a reluctant nod, trying to dismiss what she'd seen. James Benton was a jerk; it was obvious. After all, he'd stood by, silent, as her career went down the tube after her mishap with him. He could have spoken up and said that it hadn't been such a big deal after all, but he hadn't.

So why was she trying to see beyond that? Why was she recalling the hurt look in his eyes when he stumbled into the pantry?

Perhaps she wanted to believe that a man that attractive and successful could just so happen to be a great guy too. What difference did it make? She'd never run into him again.

"It's a good thing you never got onto the Lion's Den," Gypsy said. "He probably would have ripped your head off."

Camila shot her a look. "What do you mean? I never even tried to go on that show."

Gypsy dropped her gaze to her mug briefly before glancing back to the horizon. "Right. That's what I mean."

Camila got stuck on the comment for a beat, but pushed past it while looking out over the traffic where a man in a suit escorted an older lady across the street. See—there *were* gentleman out there. James Benton just wasn't one of them. "I swear if I ever see that guy again, I'll spit in his face."

"That's disgusting," Gypsy said. "*And* illegal. *And* something I'd be *way* more likely to do than you." She bit at her thumbnail before lifting her hand and inspecting it. Blue and green polish covered alternate nails, matching the two locks of colored hair in her otherwise platinum bob. "Plus, you're too much of a professional to do anything like that."

Camila couldn't argue. "Well, I'd *feel* like it," she assured. The truth was, her grandparents had raised her better than that. She'd never say or do anything to jeopardize her reputation or the career she'd worked so hard for. It just sucked that a perfect stranger could come along and mess it up for her.

"Hey, Camila," came a deep, distant voice. "How you doing this morning?" An Italian accent coated the greeting, telling

Camila just who stood in front of her building. She tipped her head slightly to get a better look at him.

Chase Marino stood there, looking suave as ever in his gray Dockers, black button-up shirt, and that ever present gold chain peeking from the open fold. The real estate mogul—who did a whole lot of business in Camila's neighborhood—often checked in with her one way or another. Hollering at her from the sidewalk seemed to be his method of choice.

"I'm doing well, thanks," she replied with a wave.

He grinned, his bright smile countering the darkness of his hair and clothes. "Say, how about we check out that new theatre up the street. Maybe grab a bite to eat afterward?"

A familiar knot clanked against her chest at the thought of turning him down yet again. Sure, the guy's persistence paid off in his business life, but here, where romance was concerned… he was wasting his time.

"Thanks for the offer," she started to say, but then Gypsy piped up and finished.

"She'd love to."

Camila felt her eyes widen as she registered what her friend had just done.

"Nice," Chase said. "I'll call you and set it up." And then he was off, darting through a break in the traffic toward the café across the street.

"I can't believe you did that," Camila hissed.

"I can't believe you'd turn down a date with him. Chase is a decent guy. Besides, haven't you seen his billboards? He reached millionaire status. And he's crazy about you."

"The millionaire status is *exactly* what I don't like about him. Who wants to start a relationship with things so…off balance?"

"Oh, so you'd like it better if you were *both* poor?"

Camila rolled her eyes. "I'm not poor. Okay, maybe I am. But—" A small buzz came from her phone where it rested beside her coffee mug. She glanced at the name on the screen as she snatched it up.

Please say she has another job offer for me. She chanted those words in her head as she brought the phone to her ear, recalling the dream job Cyree had offered shortly before she retracted it. The guest—who'd requested a personal chef for his stay at the Royal Palm Resort—had canceled his trip last minute, leaving Camila scrambling for the next catering job instead.

"Cyree?" she said as she picked up the call. "How are you?"

Gypsy shuffled to the open french doors with her empty mug. "Be right back," she whispered.

"I'm good," Cyree said through the line. "And I've got some great news. The guy who wanted a personal chef for his stay— the one who canceled—just called. He sent his brother to stay at the villa, since he still had the place reserved for the month, and *he* needs a personal chef during his stay."

Camila couldn't contain the grin that crept onto her face. She recalled her first conversation with Cyree about the potential job. The details were impossible to pass up. "Same pay and everything?"

"Yep. Same pay, and you'll be staying in the Tuscany Mansion for the month."

Anticipation stirred within her as she pictured the posh resort Cyree ran in South Carolina. That mound of hope was growing once more.

"When would it start?"

"Today. And trust me, this guy has a lot of wealthy friends in your neck of the woods. It could be a great way to rebuild your clientele."

Camila glanced over her shoulder to see Gypsy at the kitchen counter, pouring cream into her tea.

"So, what's the verdict?" Cyree asked.

Anticipation stirred at her insides once more, bubbling like a cool, fizzy drink. Great pay *and* a chance to gain future clientele...Why work for the rich and famous when she could just work for the rich instead?

"It's a yes," she blurted, realizing she hadn't said it aloud. "Definitely. I'm in."

"Perfect. I'll book the next flight leaving LAX and text you the details. We'll have a car ready to pick you up at the airport when you arrive. Oh, and I'm sending over a pantry list of food items. Check the boxes you'd like, add anything we might have missed, and we'll have the kitchen fully stocked by the time you arrive. You'll be cooking for the both of you. However, he'll take his meals alone."

Alone? "Is this business or pleasure?"

"Can't say," Cyree said. "Could be either. Everyone's idea of vacationing is different."

"That's true." Camila pushed her other questions aside. "Just wondering. The job sounds perfect."

"Sweet!" Cyree said. "Get ready to come on out."

A burst of excitement shot through her, pulse rushing like the distant tide as she set her phone back onto the table. She could hardly wait to get back to work in the kitchen. Preparing her own creations. It's what she loved most.

"What did I miss?" Gypsy asked, steadying her steaming mug. A fresh tea tag dangled from one side.

Camila caught a hint of the minty scent and smiled. "I just accepted a job offer. Turns out that super rich guy I was going to work for has a brother who's taking his place at the resort."

"The billionaire? Bam!" Gypsy thrust a palm toward her, and Camila reached up to give her a high five. "That's what I'm talking about!" She started bringing her mug to her lips, but stopped suddenly and lowered it once more. "Are you sure you're not going to be working for Mr. Yolk-on-his-diamond-crusted-cufflinks? *He's* got wealthy brothers."

Camila rolled her eyes. "I'm sure. The resort is clear on the other side of the country. East coast."

"Wow! The job goes until the end of the month. You get twenty-eight days with a billionaire. That's...pretty cool."

Camila shrugged, recalling the trip Gypsy had ahead of her. "And *you'll* be spending twenty-one days doing yoga in the Bahamas."

Gypsy let out a long, wistful sigh. "Yes, I will. Hey, you said this villa is in some sort of resort. Which one is it?"

Camila considered all the hype surrounding the world famous resort. A place big names from all over the world spent time in the sun and sand. She gave her a wide grin, allowing herself to enjoy the idea of it herself. "Ever heard of the Royal Palm?"

CHAPTER 4

*T*all, leafy trees lined the private, winding drive leading to the properties at the Royal Palm. Just moments ago, Camila had enjoyed the sights of the afternoon sun glistening off the ocean tide. Bright umbrellas shaded welcoming chairs along the beach, and Camila couldn't help but imagine reclining on one with a good book.

Yet here in the wooded parts of the property, there was no sign of the beach. Each massive mansion was hidden by hills, valleys, hedges, and trees. A blanket of English ivy covered the ground and even climbed up several tree trunks too. Camila had never witnessed so much green all in one place.

"This is beautiful," she said in a whisper.

Kyler, a driver for the resort, blew out a whistle. "You can say that again. It's not often I drive into these parts. The guests usually bring in their own drivers. Wonder who you're going to be cooking for," he added.

Camila grinned. During the short drive, the two had developed a kinship of sorts. Both working in the service industry as they did. Often working for the wealthy.

"Me too," she said. "Someone who wants his privacy, that's all I can say. That contract I signed was—"

"Crazy?" He tipped his head. "They're freaking paranoid if you ask me. All of them. Not like we're hiding royalty here or something."

Camila lifted a brow. "But maybe we are…"

"Guess you're right. Not that you'll be able to tell me if you are." Kyler pulled into a narrow drive and stopped beneath a canopy of leafy branches.

Camila ducked to peer into the clearing through the window. There, she finally caught a glimpse of the mansion. Rustic rock accented the massive stucco structure. Ornate fountains and ironwork enhanced a theme that had her picturing Spanish vineyards and glasses of wine. "Wow," she breathed.

"They don't call it the Tuscany Villa for nothing," Kyler said.

The ground cover on the outskirts of the mansion was different than what she'd spotted along the way, the ivy being replaced by a blended use of tile, rock, and clay colored gravel. Potted plants and marble statues added to the appeal. She half expected a team of viola players to greet her as she stepped out of the town car.

"This is honestly one of the most beautiful places I've ever seen," she said. Sure, Shimwah's mansion was impressive. Very. And so were the others she'd served in. But so many of them lacked character. More cold and sterile. New looking, not eclectic.

"Yeah," Kyler said as he climbed out of the car. "And this is just the back of the house." He opened Camila's door and offered his hand. "My mom would *love* to stay at this place."

She took his hand after gathering a few of her things, then walked to the back of the town car for her luggage. "Cyree told me to go ahead and enter through the upper deck in back. Guess it leads right to the kitchen."

"Sounds good. I'll carry your things for ya," Kyler offered.

Camila almost told him not to bother, but as she juggled her purse, sunglasses, house key card, and carry-on bag, she figured she may as well let him get her large suitcase up the steps. And what a gorgeous case of stairs they were. Stained stone lined with clay pots and flowering plants.

"I'll be happy to take you to the market for any food items you might need," he assured. "Cyree said she gave you my number?"

Camila nodded. "Yes. And she also had the kitchen and pantry stocked during my flight. We should be good for a while, but I'll let you know. Thank you." She spun around as Kyler reached the top of the stairs behind her. "I can take it from here," she said with a nod.

"I guess this is as good as place as any." Kyler set the suitcase onto its wheels and nodded to the french doors. "I hear they've got these crazy blinds that shut out all the sunlight and make it feel like night when it's day."

"Huh. Who would want that?" she asked, realizing she couldn't see past the glass.

Kyler shrugged. "That's a good question. You got the key?"

She slipped her sunglasses onto the top of her head and held up the card with a grin. "Got it."

Kyler held her gaze for a blink, something in his eyes

causing a stir of warmth to surge through her. He was attractive, she realized, admiring his kind eyes and finely trimmed beard. He was younger than her, probably nineteen or twenty, while Camila had hit her mid-twenties just a month ago.

"Thank you, again," she said. "I'll um…reach out when I need you."

"Please do," he said with another nod, then hurried back down the steps.

Camila was about to wave the key card over the lock pad when she caught a glimpse of her reflection in the tall glass door. *Oh.* She should definitely check to make sure she looked all right.

A quick step back allowed her to see from the tips of her highlighted hair to the sandals she wore on her feet. She'd decided on khaki, knee-length shorts, her cream-colored button-up blouse, and her favorite gold chain, which may as well be tattooed on her since she rarely parted with it.

She reached into her purse, applied a quick coat of lip-gloss, and gave her cheeks a pinch. There—nice, presentable, and professional. The latch gave way at the magic wave of her card, and Camila wasted no time dragging her suitcase inside. But what was this? It was black as pitch.

In fact, as she closed the door behind her, the waning streak of light disappeared completely. "Guess Kyler was right," she mumbled, tugging the door back open. She used the outdoor glow to find the nearest light switch and flicked the thing on.

Bright, welcoming lights flashed into life, illuminating one of the largest kitchens she'd seen. An array of the finest industrial appliances stood beneath rustic, rock-covered arches, matching the Italian theme of the home. Stone tile flooring accented the dark glazed oak of the cabinets, while a massive slab of marble covered the center island. She counted out the number of stools tucked up to the bar and gasped as she got to eight.

She'd already been musing on certain dishes she could make, but this place was inspiring an entirely new menu. A thin herb bagel with fresh, fragrant pesto, sundried tomatoes, and slices of soft mozzarella topped with a balsamic drizzle. Or maybe a pancetta and goat cheese frittata with caramelized onion and roasted potato wedges.

Camila had texted Cyree to see if her new boss had any food allergies she needed to be aware of. He hadn't, which was wonderful. The only other thing that might interfere with the menu options was the dreaded picky eater. One guy refused to eat tomatoes in any form. No pasta sauce, pizza sauce, or even barbeque sauce, which was usually a safe one even for kids.

Please don't let him be like that.

A recollection of James Benton shot to her mind. The ridiculous way his face had scrunched up when she'd mentioned the quail egg. "What a jerk," she mumbled under her breath. And just why couldn't she leave the incident in the past where it belonged? It happened—so what? Did that mean she had to relive it time and time again, make herself sick over an incident that was virtually beyond her control?

Enough already.

From this moment on, Camila would vow to keep that part of her past in the past. She sucked in a deep breath and made a slow circle around the kitchen that put her prior dream kitchen to shame. Several unique details added to the appeal.

The mortar and rustic bricks supporting the archways and

edges. The charming copper hood over one of the stoves. And what was this? A pot filler—one of those long, retracting faucets tapped right into the wall high enough to fill the tallest pot; she'd always wanted one in her own kitchen.

A rush of gratitude swept through her. And excitement too. Her time here would be prosperous, she'd see to that, but she'd also take time to enjoy the sights, sounds, and aromas along the way.

Tonight she'd prepare a classic: *carrillada de cordero*—Braised Iberian Pork Cheek with Port Wine and Honey. She could almost smell the rich, savory flavors of the sauce as she sautéed the shallots, peppers, and onions.

Now to see if her new employer was here.

"Excuse me," a voice came from behind. He'd spoken low so as not to startle her, she could tell by the tone, but it had made her jump all the same.

Camila pressed a hand to her heart and gasped. "You scared me," she breathed while spinning in place.

"My apologies," the man added to it, but Camila was too distracted by the shocking sight before her to even hear what he was saying. Dark hair, blue eyes, and well defined jawline. While all those things were adding up to a familiar face, it was the brooding look in his brow that made it official.

Her body reacted before her brain. Face warming. Chest tightening. Pulse crouching at the startup line, ready to bolt at the gunshot.

And the trigger? The one and only Mr. James Benton.

He stood at the other end of the kitchen, mumbling something or other.

"I'm sorry." She shook her head, hoping to snap out of the

horrendous nightmare unfolding before her eyes. Her hands felt prickly and hot. Her throat was threatening to close in on her.

If this really was the man she thought it was...

If he was saying anything *other* than *I'm so sorry for screwing your life up and I want to make up for it somehow*, she'd need a chair to sit on or a punching bag to attack, preferably one shaped like the Benton brother who'd ruined her life.

"Could you, umm...repeat that?" she managed.

He did a lazy looking, one-shoulder shrug. "I asked if you were the housekeeper. I'm in need of—"

"Whoa, whoa, whoa!" Camila put her hand up as a firebomb went off in her chest. "What you're *in need of* is some manners, Mr. Benton. And apparently a pair of eyes that actually see beyond people who rank in your own financial status."

His blue eyes widened. The clash of shock and confusion playing over his face might have been comical if it wasn't so infuriating.

"Are you *really* trying to act like you don't recognize me?" She kept a fixed glare on his eyes as they narrowed in concentration.

He shook his head absently. "*Should* I?"

One hard laugh sounded in her throat. "Wow. I guess that depends. If you claim to be a decent human who recognizes the wrong he's done to a *fellow* human, then yeah, you should definitely recognize me." She'd barely gotten the words out with as frazzled as she felt. This had to be an alternate universe. There was no way this was real.

But it was. And Camila wasn't about to stick around for... whatever the month might entail. "You can find somebody else to play your little games, sir. I've got better things to do with my time." She spun on one heel before casting a glance at her luggage; she couldn't leave that behind.

"Please, wait—" he said calmly. "I honestly do not know what you're talking about."

If he even knew how angry that made her, he wouldn't keep on repeating it. Or maybe he would. But she wouldn't give him the satisfaction of seeing how riled she was. She grabbed onto her suitcase handle, hiked the straps of her purse and travel bag onto her shoulder and grunted as she tipped the heavy case. The wheels wobbled and squeaked as she hobbled to the door. A door James Benton beat her to.

He blocked it off with his tall frame and folded his arms. "I'm not going to force you to stay, obviously—"

"You couldn't do that if you tried."

"But I *am* asking that you engage in a civilized conversation about what I did to offend a woman I've never met."

"If you say you've never met me again I'm going to slap you." *Oh, Lord. Please say no one was recording this anywhere.* If grave-rolling was a real thing, her grandparents were doing it for sure.

His sapphire eyes stayed locked on hers, but a hint of amusement lit his expression. The surprised-looking lift of his brow. The smallest tug at one corner of his mouth. He closed his eyes and blew out a pursed breath. Not amused—*angry.* He was having to calm himself down, was he? Welcome to the club, buddy.

"Forgive me," he said, his tone low and steady. "I don't remember meeting you, and it's obvious that I've offended you, so would you do me the honor of explaining that before you leave me to fend for myself for the month?"

Camila steadied her suitcase with shaky hands, then matched his posture with folded arms of her own. He'd almost sounded apologetic. *Almost.*

"Is that all you're worried about? Having to fend for yourself if I leave?"

He shook his head. "No. It bothers me that I upset you—a great deal, it seems—and I don't even know how or when. I think it's more likely you encountered one of my brothers and are confusing me with—"

She shook her head, unable to let him finish. "You're James, right?"

He stopped short. Nodded. "Yes, I am."

"That's what I thought. It's you. And let me start by—"

"May we please have a seat before discussing this further?" He waved an arm toward a dining area around the corner.

The adrenaline surging through her was hard enough to contain while she stood on her feet. "No."

The heart pounding increased as she awaited his reaction.

He appeared calm, Camila would give him that much. But even still, she detected a fresh hint of surprise on his face. Another breath pushed slowly through his lips before he continued. "I find it's better to do business if—"

"We're not doing business, okay? I've never worked for you. I don't *intend* to work for you. What I'd like to do is refresh your memory." She held her breath for a blink, released a deep exhale, and gave him a hint. "Mr. Shimwah's party—we bumped into each other on his back patio steps."

She studied his face as he took in her words, waiting for a flash of enlightenment.

At last, it came. A fresh glint sparked in his blue eyes.

He pointed at her. "Quail eggs."

"That's right." She might feel a level of satisfaction, but Mr. Benton didn't look the least bit sorry. He looked more pleased with himself for remembering.

His chest and shoulders puffed as he nodded. "Yes, I remember now. That was a great meal, actually. You're a talented cook."

Camila's lips were parted and poised for her next words. Words that evaporated before she could even speak them. Her thoughts bounced back to the social media posts. "If you think so, you should tell your *girlfriend* that. She posted about me that night, in case you didn't know, and made me look like a total idiot. I'm still trying to recover."

His gaze shifted for a beat, taking her in from head to toe. An odd dose of heat skittered over her skin as he met her eyes once more.

"I didn't know that," he said, voice raspy.

Grandma used to say Camila possessed a secret talent—one that was nearly foolproof: she could spot a lie from a mile away. And as she tuned into those senses, catching the sincerity in his blue eyes, Camila detected truth in his words. In fact, she'd bet his billions that he truly didn't know about the posts.

"Listen," he said, putting his arms up to either side of him. "I apologize for any part I might have played in Adel's post. Let me make it right by employing you this month. If the food at Shimwah's is any indication, I'm sure I'll be pleased with your services, and I can make a public recommendation online." He tipped his head a bit.

"Well, have my PA post it from my account since I'm no good at that stuff."

Camila felt her shoulders loosen, the tension seeming to drain from them as she considered his offer. "That would be nice."

She remembered thinking he was attractive when he wandered into the pantry at the dinner party. That attraction or anything resembling it had vanished upon his outburst on the steps. Adel Bordeaux's posts had made the two of them seem downright ugly from her perspective.

But in that moment, with the powerful billionaire just steps away from her, Camila felt that attraction creeping in once more. She gulped as her cheeks flushed warm. "I won't stay if your girlfriend's going to be here."

"She won't."

"Not even for a visit?"

Another two steps brought him even closer. Had she realized he was so tall?

He dropped his arms to his sides. "Not even for a visit."

A new level of relief swept through her. Maybe this was doable after all.

"So?" Mr. Benton stretched a hand toward her. "You'll stay?"

Camila went over the payment in her mind, adding his promise to the mix. Having his recommendation would go a long way. Heck, it'd be coming from the very guy she'd spilled the dumb quail egg on to begin with; what was better?

At last she managed a stiff nod as she reached to shake his hand in return. "Yes, I'll stay."

The brooding furrow in his brow smoothed a bit. "Now," he said, "let's try this again, shall we? I'm James Benton. And you are…" He lifted his chin as he drifted off.

"Camila Lopez." She firmed up another handshake, since he still hadn't let go of her hand.

"Camila," he said with a nod.

The sound of her name in his deep, powerful voice caused warmth to circle her heart. Very few people pronounced her name with the accent. She liked the way he had.

"It's late," he said. "Why don't I fend for myself this evening, and we can start fresh in the morning?"

"If that's what you'd like." She tried to hide the disappointment she felt at his request; she was anxious to get cooking. It was what she was there for, after all.

Only then did he release her hand, almost hesitantly, before spinning around to scan the counter top. The spicy scent of his cologne stirred in the air.

"I swear I saw fruit in here somewhere…" He moved over to the entrance where Camila had found the light switch, and turned on more lights. She took a few steps to watch as he walked over to the breakfast bar and snatch a green apple out of a wooden bowl.

He looked over his shoulder, lifted a brow, then tossed the apple in the air before catching it. "Bon appetite." He took a big bite and headed into the foyer.

Anger still brewed beneath the surface, but as Camila watched James Benton stride out of the room, inhaling hints of that heavenly cologne even still, a spark of excitement sparked up as well. The next twenty-eight days were sure to be interesting.

CHAPTER 5

*J*ames frowned as he tapped on the keyboard. He'd promised himself he'd leave his laptop alone, yet here he was, wasting the evening away trying to get on some stupid social media network.

He shook his head while staring at the bright screen. The cursor blinked, taunting him as he racked his brain. "Give it one last try..." he mumbled, typing the name of his first pet—a gerbil named Frank—followed by a one, a two, and a three. He punched the return button, irritation flaring as he watched the circle spin.

Password failed.

James groaned. "You've got to be kidding." He hadn't wanted to bother Stephanie so soon, but desperate times called for desperate measures. He grabbed his temporary cell phone (he'd left his personal cell back home) and dialed the only number programmed in the thing.

"Miss me so soon?" she asked.

"How do I log into my account?"

"Hello to you too. And which account is it?"

James hesitated; he didn't want Stephanie making a big deal of things. *Things* being the situation with his personal chef. An image of the strong-willed woman shot to his mind. Gorgeous olive skin, cheeks flushed pink with anger as she basically told him off. Something he wasn't used to.

James Benton lived in a world where most people bent down to kiss the ground he walked on. Whether they wanted his money or his acceptance or both, he rarely knew or cared. But this woman seemed perfectly content to forgo both, meaning she'd forgo a job that would pay her better than anything she was likely to find. A job that would allow her to spend the next month in a luxury mansion on one of the finest beaches in the country. Was he really that repugnant?

"James?" Stephanie trilled. "What account are you trying to log into?"

He cleared his throat. "MyBook."

"MyBook?" she said like it was a dirty word. "Why?"

James rolled his eyes. "You opened the account for me, right?"

"Right, but—"

"Then please just tell me what password I need so that I can log in already."

"Fine." Okay, so maybe Stephanie mouthed off to him every once and a while, but he was glad about that. He couldn't have a personal assistant who catered to feelings over his wellbeing or that of his business.

"It's Bowie321."

His face scrunched up. "Huh. That doesn't sound remotely familiar." Sure, he was a Bowie fan, but who wasn't?

He typed out the characters in the open space and smacked the return key once more. The circle spun, the screen went black, and at last, revealed his MyBook profile.

"Ah," he mumbled. "Sweet success." James scrolled down to see a few of the updates Stephanie had posted for him. The latest ones encouraged viewers of The Lion's Den to tune into their special live episode. He resisted the urge to click on those posts, realizing they'd probably garnered a fair share of angry comments after his outburst last night.

"Did it work?" Stephanie asked.

"Mmm, hmm..." It was all he could muster while typing Adel's name into the search bar. He hit return, found her verified page, and flinched as he saw how many times the woman posted in a given day. And she, unlike him, was the one behind the updates.

Killing it at my shoot in Mazatlan, she boasted on a beach photo of her in a bikini. She was gorgeous, James would give her that much, but Adel hadn't tapped into his heart just yet. He wasn't sure any woman would. Heck, he hadn't really crushed on a girl since his freshman year in college, and even then, he'd been compelled to leave it at that—a crush from afar.

James had known early on that finding a self-sufficient woman was the only way to weed out the ones more attracted to his bank account than they were him. But finding a woman in that category who had the other qualities he was looking for was proving a difficult task.

He scrolled past what seemed to be endless posts of Adel at

her shoots and he recalled a detail that might help him find what he was looking for.

"You there, Stephanie?"

"Yes, Mr. Silent. I am."

He readied his fingers on the keyboard once more. "Can you give me the exact date of Ricco Shimwah's dinner party, please?"

She did, and James wasted no time locating the post in question.

"Shimwah's party might have been perfect if it hadn't been for the clumsy cook who spilled raw egg on my date, @JamesBenton. Let's show @CamilaCooks that it's uncool to act a fool!"

He cringed, a sharp prick of heat stabbing at his chest. Beneath the post were comments including the video footage Camila spoke of. People reenacting the encounter, each blowing it out of proportion to a massive degree. No wonder she was so ticked off.

"This is pretty ugly." He hadn't exactly realized he'd said it aloud until Stephanie spoke up.

"Adel's post bashing the personal chef?" she asked.

"You *knew* about this?"

"*Everybody* knew about it. You deal with famous people, you have to be ready for the wrath that comes with it, if you ask me."

James wasn't surprised by Stephanie's less-than-sympathetic reply; she'd had her fair share of cruel clients and hard knocks before he'd hired her. She'd overcome them, and he admired her for it. But that didn't stop the sharp pain from sinking deeper. He didn't like that this had happened to Camila. And with his name attached.

"It was an innocent mistake," he said. "We ran into each other. Heck, it was probably more my fault than it was hers. I was…not in a good headspace."

"Why do *you* care about this all of the sudden?"

James shot to his feet, paced from his office desk and into the adjoining master suite. "Why *wouldn't* I care, Stephanie? Just what kind of person do you think I am?"

Camila's words came back to him with an added sting. *If you're a decent human who recognizes the wrong he's done to a fellow human…you should definitely recognize me.* Yet he hadn't. As inadvertent as his involvement might be, James hated that he hadn't even been aware of the damage she'd suffered.

"James?" Stephanie's voice came again.

He stopped pacing. "Yes?"

"Who exactly *is* this woman to you?"

Something about the way she'd phrased the question made him pause.

"Is *she* the chef they called in?" Stephanie guessed. "Because I'm sure we can have her replaced—"

"No," he spat. "That's not what I want at all. Don't you get it?"

Stephanie laughed. "Apparently I don't. Why don't you tell me what I'm missing here? From my perspective, you've got someone in there who's probably seeking revenge of some sort. You'll probably end up poisoned or something. Or blackmailed."

James rolled his eyes. "You've got her all wrong. And she didn't even know it was *me* until she showed up. In fact, she wanted to leave the second she saw me."

"So why didn't you let her?" Stephanie challenged.

James wasn't sure how to answer that. Only knew that he was very glad he *hadn't* let her go. "I don't know," he mumbled.

Call him weak or crazy or already-riddled-with-*enough*-guilt-from-his-brother's death, but James wanted to help repair the damage done to her reputation as a personal chef. Beyond that, he liked the idea of spending the next thirty days with her near.

She might just be his ticket to...do things he wouldn't normally do, as his brother prescribed.

His fascination went beyond her obvious beauty; that trait never had been enough to get his attention. This woman had a certain boldness about her. She was passionate. Intriguing.

"I'm worried about you," Stephanie said softly through the line. "Death dates can really throw people for a loop. When my father died—"

But James piped up before she could finish. "*My* father died too, you know?" Not that he had to remind her. "I already *know* what it's like to deal with loss. I really don't want advice and I definitely don't need pity." Agitation flared hot in his chest as he paced the length of the office.

Silence fell over the line.

A clock centered over the fireplace ticked and tocked. The last thing James needed was one more thing to apologize over.

"Hey," he finally said. "I really do appreciate your help. I think I'll call it a day."

"Are you sure you don't want me to come out there?" she asked, her voice sounding broken now. There it was—one more indication that his suspicion might be correct.

James shook his head. "You hate being out of the city, Stephanie," he reminded. "How about you take a vacation when

51

I get back? That only sounds fair." The truth was, James didn't like the idea of having even one day without his PA at his beck and call, but perhaps she needed an escape of her own.

"We can talk about it later," she said. "And um, are you feeling any better? After last night…"

It took him a moment to recall what she was referring to. "Oh, my blowup on The Lion's Den? Yes, I am." It was more of kneejerk response. When one asks how you're doing, the other answers *fine*. 'Are you feeling better?' *'Why, yes, thank you.'*

He shut his eyes and forced out a slow breath. "Thank you for asking."

"Of course," she said. "Night."

"Goodnight." He tapped the screen to end the call and folded his arms over his chest. He wasn't sure how much better he felt, but one thing could be said about James' current state of mind. He'd almost forgotten all about his troubles on The Lion's Den and the little black case he'd brought along with him. Camila had dominated his thought since his run-in with her. Something few people were capable of doing.

A series of taps sounded from behind.

He spun to see Camila standing at the open doorway, her posture guarded and unsure. Warmth rushed up his neck in a hot flash. "Yes?"

"Sorry to bother you, sir—"

"Mr. Benton," he corrected. "James, actually, if you don't mind."

The beautiful brunette pursed her lips together for a beat. "I've got a list of menu items I'm prepared to make this week. Would you mind marking the meals you're most interested in, and I'll focus on those? We'll continue the process week-by-week, and hopefully give you a good variety of dishes throughout your stay."

He nodded, though inside he was wondering just how much of his conversation with Stephanie she'd overheard. "That sounds good to me."

She stepped inside with a thin folder, flipped it open, and rested it on the desk beside his laptop.

James' pulse spiked as he considered the MyBook post on his open screen. He worked to peel his gaze off the back of the back of his laptop while he strode back toward the desk.

"Also," she said, "I was wondering which room I should stay in."

James tried registering what she'd said, but something odd had caught his attention. It seemed that for each step James took toward the desk, Camila took a backward step away from it.

The woman really did despise him, didn't she?

James pressed his laptop closed once he was settled into the office chair and forced his mind back to her inquiry about the bedrooms.

"That's a good question," he said, recalling the map Duke had told him about. The layout showed there were a number of rooms on each floor. How long had it taken her to locate him in such a place?

"I say...take the room that suits you. Whichever you'd like. And I think we should probably exchange phone numbers." Heat rushed into his face as he realized how that must have sounded. "That way you won't have to hunt me down when you need me."

Her gaze drifted to the adjoining master suite. Upon arrival,

James had opened the custom pocket doors wide to create one wide, joined space.

She cleared her throat and set her eyes back on him. "True." Her brown eyes might lack the hostility he'd seen earlier, but they were definitely guarded. Her posture was tipped away from him, toward the door, indicating just where she preferred to be.

Still, she tugged her phone from her back pocket. "Tell me your number. I'll shoot you a text so you'll have mine too."

Just why was his pulse speeding suddenly? "It's two one three…" But then he remembered about his new phone. "Actually, don't do that one. I left my personal cell behind and I haven't the slightest clue what the number to this one is."

Camila let out a sigh. "Here," she said, approaching his desk once more. *Dang*, that smile was pretty. "I'll send myself a text from yours then."

"Good idea." James set the phone on the edge of the desk rather than placing it directly in her hand. "There it is." The front of his neck burned some more as he forced his eyes to the menu. He released a pursed breath, hoping to prevent that heat from spreading to his face yet again.

He'd learned tactics to keep from getting flustered to that degree, but Camila's close proximity was making it hard. She smelled good too. *Very* good. A subtle perfume perhaps, both sweet and tangy, a combination of innocence and allure.

"I'm going to make this easy," he said while closing the leather fold. "I'll let you pick out the menu based on what you like best. How's that?" He lifted his gaze to catch her eye.

Camila tipped her head to one side. The small furrow at her

brow said she might not love the idea as much as he did. Had he offended her?

"It all looks so good," he added, holding out the menu for her.

She looked at it, tapped a few keys on his phone, and then handed it to him in exchange for the menu. "Okay." She walked toward the hallway but stopped in her tracks. "Why don't you text me the meal schedule you'd like for tomorrow."

He pointed at her. "Another good idea." Why was he being so lame? "I'll do that. Oh, and I know I didn't pick menu items or anything, but you know that beet salad you made at Shimwah's gathering?"

Her brown eyes went wide. "Yes..."

"Could you make that? I really liked it."

"Sure." Camila nodded, a bit of confusion playing over her face.

"Oh, and my private chef back at home always cuts up a watermelon for me every few days. He puts it in the fridge for me. Think you could do the same?"

She nodded. "You like watermelon?"

"Remember that school-aged joke about loving something so much you could marry it?"

Camila's brow furrowed, but she gave him another nod just the same.

"Well, yeah. That's what everyone said I should marry. Watermelon." Boy, did he sound stupid.

James wasn't sure why he wanted to keep her from going so soon. Perhaps it was to move beyond the distance she'd placed between them. Funny thing was, it was usually James who set the barriers. Tall and wide ones.

"Well," she said, smiling just enough to reveal a dimple in her cheek. A very cute dimple. "I'll have some cut up for you within the hour. Help yourself."

"Thank you," he said, feeling unsettled even still. For some reason, he wanted Camila to relax around him. To smile, maybe, over something he said. To make herself at home in the very least.

"Camila?" he blurted as something came to mind.

She glanced over her shoulder. "Yes?"

"I wanted to make sure they told you that...that I'd like you to enjoy the amenities while you're here. Not only the beach, of course, but there's a workout room, a pool out back..."

Another nod. Another perplexed expression.

"Thank you. And Cyree said there would be a housekeeper staying here as well."

Oh no, had she been planning on having a fellow service worker here with her? James raked a hand through his hair as he replied. "The housekeeper is a fulltime employee of the Royal Palm, which means she has her own living space already. Outside of the villa."

When Camila didn't respond right away, he hurried to add to it. "But she'll be in and out a few times throughout the day, so it won't *always* just be the two of us." *Shut the crud up, James!*

Her shoulders went a bit higher, tighter, as she sucked in a breath. An odd knot of concern snuck in during the quiet moment. Would she say she didn't want to stay under those conditions?

Maybe. But who cared if she did? What difference would it make to him whether she stayed or not?

Finally, she nodded, her pretty face unreadable even still.

"Okay." She spun around without another word and stepped out of the room.

James stared at the doorway moments after she left, trying to dissect what was going on with him. What was he feeling for this woman? Pity? No, he couldn't pity a woman as strong and determined as Camila seemed to be.

He shook his head, bringing his phone to eye level, anxious to see the message she'd sent herself from his phone.

This is James Benton's number, was all it said. Which made sense. Why should it say more than that? She was just getting his number in her phone. And now he had hers. Warmth stirred in his belly at the idea. He found himself wanting to know more about her. Who she was. What she was like outside of work.

The appetite that had vanished after last night's TV debacle was coming back now with a vengeance. Which reminded him, he was supposed to send her a meal schedule for tomorrow. Back at home, James had a loose version of a private chef. Mark Tosly cooked for several of the residents in his area, cooking the same meals in bulk and delivering them at set times each day. May as well stick with that one.

James: *Breakfast: 7:00 Dinner: 7:00*

He hit send, but then hurried and added to it: *Thank you, Camila.*

Camila. He liked that name. Liked the way it rolled off her tongue with that slight Spanish accent. He stared at the screen as it sent, wondering if he should say something more. He found himself wanting to tell her that he saw a few of the videos. That they were horrible, and he was sorry for being so ignorant to the ordeal.

His phone buzzed, and a spark of anticipation skittered through him.

Camila: *No lunch?*

Oh. He'd forgotten about that. James and his staff usually just had food delivered to the office, a detail Tina, his secretary, took care of.

He picked a spot in the middle of the day.

James: *How's 1:00?*

More screen-staring.

Another buzz.

Camila: *Perfect. See you in the morning.*

Yes, he would see her in the morning, and he liked that knowledge more than he should.

James sighed and sank back into the office chair. His lovely private chef should probably remain off limits, but he was breaking the rules now—Dr. Duke's orders. Rules he hadn't exactly planned to follow...until that moment.

And why not?

Camila's presence—along with the rude awakening of what had happened to her—had managed to take his mind off a situation that had haunted him since his brother's death. Already, the prescribed therapy was starting to work.

He wasn't sure what the rest of his time there would look like, but something told James this would be more than the escape he'd been looking for. Perhaps he'd actually enjoy his time at the Royal Palm.

CHAPTER 6

*C*amila might have been sleeping on a high quality mattress with the finest sheets in one of the most gorgeous homes she'd stepped foot in, but that hadn't equaled a good night's sleep.

She'd been too disturbed by her shocking run-in with James Benton. She guessed it had gone well enough, considering the circumstances. And sure, she'd trusted what he'd said while he was saying it, but the moment her new billionaire boss stepped out of the room, doubt began worming its way into her thoughts. Why had she believed her instincts were foolproof? She knew nothing about the guy. Except that he was dating the girl who was single-handedly trying to ruin her life.

Camila continued to remind herself of that very thing.

All.

Night.

Long.

She'd never been a paranoid person, but thanks to the situation with Adel, Camila now scrutinized people under a new lens, and James was no exception. In fact, during the wee hours of night, she'd even convinced herself that Adel was probably behind this whole thing, ready to film prime footage, post it on her blog, and have another laugh at Camila's expense.

The idea was farfetched at best—she realized that much in the light of day—but she couldn't quite shake the lingering doubts that clung onto her like a subconscious disease. Threatening to contaminate the impression she made on her new boss. Camila knew herself all too well. Sure, Gypsy was wild and free—she said and did things Camila would only dream of. But for all of Camila's awareness and poise, she possessed a level of passion that loosened her tongue. And unlike Miss Let-it-go-with-the-wind, Camila clung to offenses with both fists.

She sighed at the acknowledgment while reaching to unfasten her apron straps. In one quick swoop, she hung it on the hook behind the pantry door, and glanced over the kitchen once more. It was only six a.m., and already, she'd prepared the beet kraut—three full jars of it— and had it setting in the sunlight along the countertop. The kraut would have to ferment for a few days, but it'd be well worth the wait.

She'd also done the prep work for breakfast—gorgeous, sliver-thin cuts of smoked salmon with fresh dill sprigs, fragrant lemon wedges, and savory capers. She would pile it high on toasted bagels with a smear of herbed cream cheese and serve it up with an array of colorful berries and a tangy yogurt dip. A sigh slipped through her lips; food was her happy place.

If she made it quick, Camila could workout for forty minutes, take the next twenty to get cleaned up, and be back to the kitchen to serve breakfast by seven.

The house map was taped to the back of a nearby utility closet. Camila walked over to it while musing on the way Mr. Benton had requested something she'd served at the party. She'd been flattered, at first. Was glad to know he'd remembered at least something from the menu that night.

But in those dark, nighttime hours, Camila had even managed to freak herself out about that. Worrying that it meant he was simply playing dumb. That he'd known exactly who she was all along.

Either way, she mused while studying the map, Camila was determined to impress James with her food and professionalism alike.

Now where was the workout room in this place? She'd memorized the location of three spots within the Tuscany Villa so far: the kitchen, the bedroom she'd selected, and the room Mr. Benton was staying in, which opened into the spacious office she'd found him pacing in the night before.

The massive villa had three full stories and each seemed to go on for days. Luckily, a circular stairwell stood at the center of each, creating a central mark.

Bright morning sunlight poured in through the wall-sized windows as Camila traced her finger over the map. She focused on the path leading from the stairs to the gym, which— like the kitchen—was on the middle floor. *Perfect.*

She'd taken it upon herself to open the sun-blocking blinds in the main living space. It was her job, after all, to create the right ambiance for dining, and natural lighting couldn't be beat. Neither could the view from the dining area. Plus, there was a private patio just out back looking over the ocean, complete with a table and chairs for outdoor dining; she hoped he'd take advantage of it.

Ample light poured from the open doorway leading to the mansion's personal gym, letting her know the blinds had been opened there as well.

Camila followed that light, rounding the corner to step into a large room that looked more like a dance studio than a gym. Open flooring stretched clear to the spectacular view beyond the floor-to-ceiling windows. Mirrors took up the opposite side of the wall, and there, tucked into one side of the room, stood all the equipment she'd hoped to find. A treadmill, elliptical, spin bike, and an array of weights resting beside a workout bench. Yet just as she moved her gaze back toward the machines, a small movement caught her attention, followed by the metal clank of a workout bar locking back into place.

Her gaze followed the muscular arms supporting that bar before she could register who they must, in fact, belong to: James Benton. Her heart pumped a hot beat out of rhythm.

Luckily, he was lying flat on his back and unable to see her, which meant she could make a quiet escape. Camila had no intention of working out in the same space as her new boss. Especially since she still hadn't decided whether or not she trusted him.

She pulled her water bottle to her chest, spun on one heel, and cringed as her shoe squeaked against the wood floors. Her heart thudded out of beat as she lifted her other foot. She was still close to the doorway, perhaps he hadn't heard—

"Hello?"

Crap. Camila froze and clenched her eyes shut.

"Don't let me scare you away," James said when she didn't

turn around. "I'm pretty sure this place is big enough for the both of us. Plus," he said through a grunt, "I'm just about finished."

Camila spun back around to see that he was sitting up now. Recently, she'd read a line about sweat glistening off the bare chest of a hero in her novel. It hadn't exactly seemed like the best phrasing in her mind, but as James Benton came to his feet on the other side of the room, she noted how nice the light sheen contrasted the contours of his muscular chest.

Her face flushed with heat. *Wow*. He really was attractive. *Stop staring, Camila.*

She gulped. "I'll just...okay, yeah. I'll go ahead and work out in here." She nodded, forced her eyes over to the exercise equipment, and shuffled one foot forward after the next. It was then she recalled her discovery in the fridge that morning. James had already eaten nearly half of the cut up fruit she'd prepared for him. It was no wonder if he hadn't eaten any dinner. But in case that was a normal habit for him, she'd texted Cyree with a request for more watermelon.

James walked over to one of the weight-lifting setups, jostled the metal bar to adjust the weight, and then took a seat once more. She couldn't help but study his profile as he grabbed the handles and lifted his feet onto the bar. He grunted as he straightened his legs against the weight.

While stepping into his viewpoint, she scolded herself once again for staring. Especially since he'd caught her in the act. Not that his expression had changed. The muscles in his face, neck, and jaw kept tight as he started another round of presses.

Her heart was acting like she was smack in the middle of a freaking marathon already. And at the sight of some—okay, seriously gorgeous—guy without a shirt on? Gypsy always warned Camila that her dateless years would cause some sort of desperation for men in her life; she was starting to wonder if her friend had been right. This was ridiculous.

She hurried over to the elliptical, glad it wasn't too close to her new boss, and tucked her earbuds into place. A quick tap at her phone, followed by a few scrolls, led to one of her favorite playlists: All Things Bowie. *Yes.* It'd be just the incentive she'd need to keep a good cadence. Hopefully it'd distract her as well.

Yet as the next thirty minutes ticked by, Camila realized that a distraction from James Benton—while he sat right in her eye line—was impossible to achieve. It was more than just his appearance; there was something intriguing about him too. Here he was, some fairly famous billionaire with the entire world at his reach, doing normal guy stuff like working out early on a sunny day.

It was odd to see such a human side of him, she guessed. And to not only see him in something other than his usual white-collared shirt, but to see the impressive spans of his chest and muscled arms... it was messing with her mind.

It didn't help that she was still trying to digest their conversations. He seemed genuinely invested in making things right, even if he hadn't been aware of the damage done. That was encouraging.

Camila had worked with enough wealthy clients to know there were kind and cold alike, as with any monetary class. But even still, it seemed more often than not the individuals she'd worked for were selfish. They were often so consumed with the need to impress that kindness and courtesy dropped off their list of priorities.

She might be wrong, but she got the feeling that James Benton wasn't bothered with appearances in that way. And there was something else she hadn't been able to get out of her head: the way his siblings reacted to his wild outburst on The Lion's Den. Of course, if that type of behavior were commonplace for the guy, it wouldn't have made news to begin with.

Camila had been so focused on her musings she hadn't noticed that James was standing right in her eye line. He dabbed his skin with a white hand towel and waved an arm over his head.

She tugged the ear bud from one ear.

"See you at breakfast," he said.

She nodded, glad he couldn't detect the increased beating of her heart. "Sounds good." Camila was about to replace her ear buds when James spoke up once more.

"Is that Bowie I hear?"

She tipped her head to one side. "Huh?"

"I, um…" He pointed at his head. "I have really good hearing. Sounds like you're listening to David Bowie?"

"Oh," she said with a nod. "Yeah, I am."

"Nice." It was the closest thing to a smile she'd seen on the brooding man since she arrived, and Camila couldn't help but smile in return. Her heart skipped three full beats. Her cheeks were probably flaming with heat, but she could blame that on the workout easily enough.

"Okay," he said. "I'm really leaving this time." And with that, he strode out of the room.

In the seconds following, Camila tapped down the speed on the workout machine, brought a hand to her heated cheeks, and reached for her water.

A vision of Adel Bordeaux came to mind. *He's taken, Camila.* And even if he wasn't, the famous model represented the type of woman James went for.

With that thought, Camila decided that tomorrow, she'd run on the beach instead.

Camila gritted her teeth as she held the phone to her ear. She couldn't remember being so tempted to break a privacy contract in all of her life. She couldn't disclose the name of her client; the agreement she'd signed was clear. But keeping it quiet was harder than it might be due to two things.

First: She was talking to Gypsy—her best friend who could read her every thought, even over the phone.

Second: Her predicament was something they'd actually joked about. Gypsy had suggested that James Benton might be her new boss, but only because he had billionaire brothers, not because it made any practical sense.

So as she spoke with Gypsy about her new job, Camila hated being deceptive. But that's exactly what she'd had to do.

"So he's just some boring old billionaire, huh? Nothing special?" Gypsy pried for the third time.

"He likes watermelon a lot," Camila offered.

"Does he? I didn't think that was a rich person's food. It's not fancy enough."

"Well, he loves it. I'll probably have to cut up a second one by the end of the day."

"That's weird."

Camila laughed. The truth was, she kind of liked that particular trait about James. It was so…normal. But then she recalled the strange way James had dodged her since they'd run into one another at the gym. Taking both lunch and dinner in his office. Talk about spoiling any semblance of meal presentation. Plus, meals were meant to be the main event, not some side chore while slaving away at a desktop.

"You're two days into this," Gypsy said, "so you better tell me that you've already gone out to the beach at least once."

She hated admitting the answer to that. "Not yet." Camila knew Gypsy was readying to pull out the lecture card, so she was quick to add to it. "But I will. Soon. I've been busy."

"Yeah, yeah. Would you just get your butt outside and turn the camera on? I want to see what you're missing."

"What *I'm* missing?" Camila asked.

"*Yes, you,*" Gypsy said. "I might be the one stuck in LA, but you're just a few feet away from it and you're still missing out."

Camila sighed as she wiped down the counter. "Fine. Just a second." She made her way to the french doors she'd come through just the day before and squinted against the brightness of the sun. Sure, there was a lot of sunlight illuminating the kitchen now that the windows were bare, but it wasn't the same as the full, unhindered strength of the evening sun.

Sounds of the beach greeted her as well, putting a smile on her face in an instant. "Wow," she said, "I should put the camera on now so you can see the back of the house too. It's gorgeous."

She did, and Gypsy let out a gasp. "You've got to be kidding."

Camila let herself take it all in—the excitement she'd nearly forgotten at the unexpected reveal of her boss. She paused then, taking a moment to inwardly thank the dear Lord above.

"I just hope I can make a good impression," Camila said as she rounded the corner.

"You will," Gypsy assured. "And I'm sure if the guy wasn't some old geezer he'd want to marry you over it."

Camila's brow furrowed. "Did I say he was an *old geezer?*"

"Well, isn't he? Sounds like it."

She probably shouldn't have said anything. If Gypsy believed Camila was working for some old guy she wouldn't pester her about a possible romance. "Well, he's old," she lied. "But he's not *that* old…"

Her words drifted off as the ocean came into view.

Gypsy uttered something that network TV would have to bleep out. "You've got to be kidding me. *That's* in your backyard?"

A wide grin spread over Camila's face. "I guess so." Distant glances over the balcony had not done it justice. Beyond a stretch of white, shimmering sand, the crystal blue ocean pushed tide after tide onto the shore. A breeze picked up, carrying the distant caw of seagulls on its wing.

"You are the luckiest woman I know right now."

"This *is* like a dream," Camila admitted. Nearer by, potted plants accented a turquoise pool in the yard. Beach chairs and umbrellas set the stage for a day of relaxing by the poolside, which would be tempting if it wasn't for the beach just a walking distance away.

"You better get in that hot tub at *least* half the nights you're there," Gypsy said.

Hot tub? Camila had missed that, but upon further inspection, the tempting sight came into view.

"Promise me you'll get in there," her friend urged.

68

An image of sliding into that hot tub beside a very gorgeous and muscular James Benton popped into her mind. Runaway goose bumps rippled over her arms, and Camila told herself they were brought on strictly by the breeze.

"I promise," she assured.

"Why couldn't you have like, snuck me into your suitcase? Maybe I can still come out. You can keep me tucked away in one of the rooms like your little dungeon girl and no one would even know."

Camila scrunched her nose. "Dungeon girl?"

"You know what would be romantic?" Gypsy said.

"I've got to get back to work," Camila said with a groan, but she knew it wouldn't stop her friend from continuing.

"If the billionaire was like, kind of this mean awful beast at first, but then he started to get nice along the way—"

"That's enough," Camila said with a laugh. "This isn't a cartoon, okay?"

But Gypsy carried on. "And suddenly he's like this handsome prince who actually *does* have a good personality. It was just hiding beneath this mountain of hurt and fear."

"Uh huh." Camila glanced at the top of the screen to check the time. Only five o'clock.

"Think about it. You've got this king-sized mansion and it's just you and him."

"*And* a housekeeper," Camila added, recalling the sweet woman she'd met just hours ago.

"Yeah, well…" Gypsy said. "That makes the story even better. No housework for you."

Camila gave into another laugh. "Well, if that magically

starts to happen—everything that you listed off—I'll be sure to let you know."

"You better. I've got a date tonight, by the way. With this guy named Trinity. He's got dreads. Seems nice."

"That's awesome," Camila said. "Text me once you're back. Let me know how it went."

"Okay," Gypsy said. "Maybe he'll take me back to *his* mansion and I can live out the fantasy on my own."

Camila chuckled as she hurried back up the steps. "Yeah. Maybe. Talk to you later." She ended the call and folded her arms as a warm breeze rushed over her skin. Her surroundings nearly demanded she close her eyes and enjoy the moment. A full breath in, then out.

The sun was getting ready to set, and it brought on romantic images of lounging on the beach or beside the pool. Slipping into the hot tub. That final image brought James into the picture once more. Suddenly she imagined him holding her gaze, his always-serious blue eyes hooded by that brooding brow. She imagined him moving closer, sliding his hands onto her hips; she gave into the warm sensation that spilled over her at the thought.

Her eyes shot open. "Stop, Camila," she scolded under her breath. Gypsy was right, wasn't she? It had been far too long since Camila had entertained the company of a man. And now here she was, in some lonely, deprived state, fantasizing about her billionaire boss who, by the way, wouldn't want anything to do with her outside of their professional setting.

Camila pictured her last relationship. Lyle King had been a good boyfriend at first. Caring, kind, and funny. But she soon saw another side to him. A controlling side. It had her musing on the hidden darkness in her past—the reason she'd been raised by her grandparents, not her parents.

It had taken years for Grandma and Grandpa Lopez to confess the details. In fact, they'd only done so after Camila dug into online articles and found out for herself what had happened. Found out that her own father was, in fact, a monster.

No, Camila. Don't reopen that wound. She'd spent years seeing a good therapist to sort through that trauma, and even still, without the love and example of her grandparents, she might not have made it through.

But that didn't erase the looming question in the back of her mind: was she—like her mother—attracted to the wrong sorts of men? Her ex boyfriend was a powerful man. A successful lawyer who earned admiration while demanding respect.

James Benton was a similar sort. At least, he seemed to be. And yet he was the only man Camila had found herself drawn to in months. Of course, that didn't mean he was anything like Lyle, or her father for that matter. Besides, she reminded herself, the topic was moot. James had a girlfriend. And even if he didn't, he would never date someone like her. Which was just fine—she wasn't interested in him either.

Camila would focus on her job and do her best to stop the daydreams before they got carried away.

CHAPTER 7

*J*ames woke up with thoughts of the Latin beauty on his mind. Before running into her in the workout room yesterday, he'd planned to apologize to her and start fresh. Instead, he'd caught himself daydreaming about a private cruise with Camila by his side, enjoying their shared taste in music. It'd been enough to scare him into hiding the entire day.

But today would be different. He'd go right back to his no-work policy and doing whatever it was he *wouldn't* normally do.

He settled on a pair of khaki slacks and a V-neck tee shirt. A quick dab of aftershave followed by a second glance in the mirror, and he was ready for his seven o'clock breakfast. One he *wouldn't* take in his room.

Just as he made his way toward the kitchen, James' phone buzzed.

Please don't be Stephanie. He tugged the small device from his pocket, and smiled when he saw the text was from Camila instead.

Camila: *Wondered if you'd like to have breakfast outside this morning? It's gorgeous out on the deck.*

Great. She probably worried that he was a total shut-in. He stopped walking and typed out a reply.

James: *Sure. Sounds nice.*

He slid the phone back into his pocket and took the wide corner, knowing Camila would likely be standing just yards away from him in the kitchen.

She was beside the counter, a fitted apron pulled over her curvy figure.

He slowed his steps as he watched her retrieve his text. A smile pulled at her lips. A broad, beautiful smile that made heat flare low in his belly. And there was that dimple. Heaven help him, but did his knees actually feel like they might give way like the old cliché implied?

Good heavens, get it together. You're James Freaking Benton.

He puffed his shoulders and wiped the dopey grin off his face. "Morning," he said with a nod.

She glanced up, her gaze drifting before settling right on him.

His pulse kicked up a notch. Her eyes were hypnotic. Even from a distance, those dark brown depths drew him in. But he'd be lying if he said they weren't guarded too.

"Good morning. Glad you said yes about the patio. Go ahead and have a seat out there. I'll, um..." She dropped her gaze back to the countertop. "Bring out your breakfast in just a minute."

An idea came to him then. A very foolish, very tempting

idea. And before he could silence it in a flash of *Regular James* sanity, he gave into it instead. "Would you like to join me?"

He couldn't exactly see her expression, with her chin down as it was, but he definitely spotted the surprised lift of her eyebrows.

His pulse grew loud and heavy at his left temple.

Camila balanced a sprig of green onto the iced drink before her, then dried her hands off with her apron. "I'm not sure—" she started to say, lifting her gaze once more, but James spoke up again.

"No pressure. I just...at some point, I'd like the chance to clear the air, if you don't mind." He despised the desperation boiling beneath his own words. Hoped she couldn't detect it for herself.

She gave him a nod, but the tightness in her expression remained. "Sure," she said. He might see more enthusiasm if she'd been summoned to jury duty during Christmas break. "Of course," she added. "Why don't you go ahead and take a seat. I'll be out in a moment."

"Very well." *Yes.* Victory. A small one, but he'd take it. He made his way to the bright patio, eyeing the table and chairs. Swooshing sounds of the lapping ocean waves urged him to relax as he lowered himself into the only chair facing the beach, but he stood back up in a blink.

Camila should have the view. He moved to the other side, putting his back against the ocean. *Wait,* that was weird too. If he moved to a side chair, they could both enjoy the view.

A quick glance told him Camila was already heading his way, tray in hand. James scooted his chair back, moved into one of the side chairs, and rolled his shoulders to ease the tension.

She kept her eyes trained on the tray as she slid it onto the table. "Here we go," she said, placing a delicious looking breakfast plate before him. "Avocado toast with poached eggs, yellow pear tomatoes, and crisp hash browns." She slid a bowl of watermelon beside it. "And a side of your favorite—fresh watermelon."

"This looks amazing. Thank you."

Camila nodded as a playful smile pulled at her lips. "Looks like I missed a good game."

James racked his brain. "Game?" Her comment made him worry that he'd missed the Dodgers game, but that wasn't on until tonight.

A small laugh sounded in her throat. "I was talking about the musical chairs you were playing out here a second ago. Looked like fun."

His face went hot. "Oh," he said, shaking his head. "Yeah, I was trying to find the best way for us to both see the ocean. This works, right?" He motioned to the chair across from him.

Camila held his gaze with a questioning look. "Yes," she said. "Thank you."

She set the other plate and fruit bowl in place, then did the same with the drinks. "This is freshly squeezed lime juice, sparkling ginger ale, and peppermint leaves. It's one of my favorites. To me, it tastes like..." She paused there, seeming to look for the right word. "It's like summertime on ice. Crisp, invigorating, and just plain happy."

"Well, with a sales pitch like that, how could I refuse?"

Camila grinned.

"No, really," he continued. "I think at this point, even if I were allergic to limes, ginger, *and* mint, I'd still probably taste it just to see what all the fuss was about."

That earned a laugh from her. "I know I get passionate. I can't help it."

He didn't want her to try; it was the very quality that drew him to her. He brought the iced glass to his lips and glanced up to see her watching him. At last he took a pull from the straw. She wasn't kidding. The flavors were tart and sweet all at once. And the mint, it seemed to make the crisp drink taste even colder.

"I have to say…it's worth the praise."

She gave him a rather humble looking nod. "Thank you."

Just what was it about this woman that made her so easy on the eyes? Her complexion was hard to ignore, the way her olive skin glowed in the sunlight. Her cheekbones were high, but not sharp like Adel's. It was a softer look. And while her almond eyes were kind and innocent, they held hints of mischief too. The best part about them is they smiled right along with her, a sight that made his pulse rev like a jet at takeoff.

James tore his gaze off her and focused on his plated meal. He used his knife to cut into the avocado toast and took his first bite. The flavor, rich and savory, was accented by something he couldn't place. He only knew it gave the dish an extra kick. He took two more bites before speaking up once more.

"This is great. Really." He wasn't exactly used to complimenting the chef; Mark usually headed to his next job as James sat up to the table, but the compliment was sincere.

"Thank you," Camila said before biting into a piece of cantaloupe. "I always squirt lemon juice over the avocado. Seems to really enhance the flavor."

"It does," he agreed. He also liked the assortment of seeds she sprinkled over the dish. Roasted sunflower and pumpkin seeds adding the perfect crunch.

It remained quiet, save the sounds of the ocean, while James finished the main course. Yet as he moved onto the fruit, spearing a piece of watermelon with his fork, he decided it was time to confront the less-than-savory topic of Adel's post.

"After we talked—upon your arrival, that is—I took it upon myself to find the post you mentioned." At the mere words, a few of the cruel comments shot to his mind. "It was horrible. I'm ashamed to admit that I was ignorant to it for so long."

Camila lifted her chin to look at him, and a dose of heat flooded his chest. She held his gaze, searching his face with a subtle nod. A loud bird cawed in the distance.

James shifted in his seat, leaning to rest his forearms on the table. "What Adel said was careless, unnecessary, and frankly, inaccurate." He shook his head. "And then her *faithful followers* had to jump on board and push things to a new level."

"Yeah," she said, tucking a strand of hair behind one ear. "They really did. I'd been cooking for Ricco Shimwah for months before that happened. But then he canceled the jobs he had scheduled, and he hasn't called me since."

A mean ache sank into his gut. Adel was oblivious.

"I'm sorry." James remembered being drawn to the popular model at first, the way she easily dismissed what others thought about her; he'd found it refreshing. But it was events like these that opened his eyes. Adel didn't care about others. She only cared about boosting her own image and career.

"You called her my girlfriend, and I allowed for that since we've let the public believe we're together, but we're not. I've never been in a committed relationship with Adel. And after this, I'll make sure the public knows that too." Boy, did he like saying that aloud. James might not be the softest peach on the tree, but he refused to be associated with someone so vicious. Or to let the public think he was into women like Adel.

He also wanted to help Camila recover from the incident. "I should be able to help you rectify the Shimwah situation soon," he said, daring himself to share a little something of his own. "I'm trying to go off the grid for while, as much as I can, anyway. Not sure if you heard about my blowup on live TV."

He watched her face for signs of enlightenment. "Did you hear about it?" he added.

"Yes." Camila dropped her gaze back to her fruit. Using the prongs of her fork, she pushed past a piece of cantaloupe, pierced a chunk of honeydew, and brought it to her lips. She didn't have watermelon in hers, he realized. Was that because she was reserving it for him, or that she didn't prefer it?

He pushed the inquiry aside. "I don't usually behave that way," he felt the need to say.

Camila nodded, covering her mouth as she finished chewing. "I could tell."

He perked up. "Have you watched other episodes?"

"No. And I didn't technically watch *that* one, either. My friend showed me the clip. But if it was normal behavior for you, it wouldn't have made news, right? Plus, I could tell by the shock on your siblings' faces. They were worried about you."

She'd said that his siblings were worried about him, but by the look on her face, he'd say that Camila was too.

James clenched his eyes shut and turned his face toward the ocean breeze. "I don't want anyone worrying about me." He felt vulnerable then. Exposed. Less the billionaire with little care and more…more a man who was seeking a mere stranger's approval. And he was. There was no denying it. James very much wanted Camila to like him. Respect him. To see sides to him other than the ugly one she'd seen when he plowed into her on the stairs. He wondered if he should tell her the truth about that night. He'd been reckless and rude, but it hadn't been for no reason at all. James had been struggling in those moments.

No. That was none of her business. But the desire was there all the same. A new flash of heat pushed through his insides. What was wrong with him? He had the sudden impulse to shoot to his feet, thunder down the stairs to the beach, and leave the conversation behind.

He glanced back to Camila, figuring she wouldn't mind if he did. The professional boundary was thinning at best. James paid his service workers well for several good reasons, one of which was to compensate for the impersonal relationship he kept with them. So why had he been so anxious to breech his code of conduct with Camila? Because of Duke and his dumb advice?

Thank her for breakfast and leave, James. Now.

His pulse sped as he entertained doing just that. His lips parted, a breath rushed in, and words tumbled off his tongue on their own accord. "Do you mind if I ask what inspired you to go into this line of work?"

If his question surprised her, she didn't show it. She did however, tilt slightly toward the breeze, allowing it to toss the strands of her hair off her shoulders. The whooshing tide grew louder, but not loud enough to stop James from berating himself for what he was doing.

Meanwhile, the other side of him was poised at the edge of his seat, curious to know about the personal chef who'd dared confront him so boldly that first day. He couldn't remember a woman putting him at war with himself in such a way.

"My grandmother was an excellent cook," Camila said, a soft smile at her full lips. "She taught me to make some of her favorite dishes while I was quite young. Ten, eleven, maybe. And it was a good thing she did, too, since her health started to deteriorate when I was fifteen; she had a severe case of muscular dystrophy."

"That's terrible." And it was, yet something good was happening too. She was opening up to him. Perhaps if he could uncover the mystery behind her, the draw would be gone. Like smoke after a magic trick. *Poof.*

Camila pulled her gaze off the beach to look at James. "I watched the food network obsessively, but it was more than just entertainment for me. It was an education. I took notes. Colorful ones, thanks to the markers, notepads, and stickers my grandfather bought in support of my addiction." She let out a short, quiet laugh. "He used to watch them with me."

James gave into a wistful grin of his own, picturing the scene for himself. The image brought a question to mind: Had Camila been raised by her grandparents?

"Anyway," she said, "that's how it all started. Eventually I went to culinary school—one of the top-rated in the country—which only fed my passion. It's like they say, the more you know, the more you realize how much there is to learn." She leaned in as her eyes widened. "And don't you think food is amazing? We eat three times a day—that gives us three different opportunities to put more joy into our lives."

She was really coming to life now. Flushed cheeks, a lively spark in her pretty eyes. Her energy was contagious, too. He couldn't ignore the stir it caused low in his gut and high in his chest. He was drawn to Ms. Camila Lopez, there was no denying it. An acknowledgment that caused an equal flash of fear.

"Sorry," she said with a sigh. "I could talk food all day."

"Don't apologize," he said. "I like it."

Camila held his gaze, fanning that clash of fear and desire within him. Call him crazy, but he could swear that the guard behind those deep brown eyes was fading fast. At the mere thought, his own guard dropped as well.

A tempting swirl of warmth stirred in his belly once more.

"I can see why you're so good at what you do," he said. "It's your passion that sets you apart."

She gave him a soft smile. "Thank you." Camila glanced toward the house, indicating she was probably wanting to get back to work. No problem, he'd done enough boundary pushing for one day. If he had half a brain left, James would take his meals in the office from here on out; it would keep him from giving in to whatever pull he felt toward her.

"So what about you?"

Camila's question caught him off guard; he was certain she was looking for a way out of their conversation.

"What was that?"

"What about your occupation?" she said. "Did you wake up one day and decide you were going to become a billionaire or what?"

For the second time during their conversation, James mused Camila was warming up to him. Her posture had definitely relaxed. And when she reached for her glass, she leaned over the table once more, closer to him.

"My story's a little different, I guess. We understood from a young age that we'd inherit our first million when we turned eighteen years old."

Camila blew out a whistle. "Happy Birthday."

He gave into a grin. "*Indeed.* But there was a second offer where that gift was concerned. If we agreed not to spend it for the first year, and to invest it as my father stipulated, we'd get an *extra* million as well as the gain made from the investments. We just had to wait until we were nineteen."

Her eyes widened. "Wow. That's...so did anyone do it? Take the one million at eighteen instead?

A vision of the black leather case weaseled into his mind at her question. "Yes." It came out in a whisper, so he cleared his throat and tried again. "My late brother, Winston, took the one mill. From the time he hit puberty, Winston had this need to show everyone that he was something special. He was out to prove, mainly to my dad, I think, that he could be successful while doing the exact opposite of what *he* would do or suggest."

James slid a thumb down the side of his glass while he spoke, sending the condensation to the base. "I never understood that about him. If you want to achieve success in a certain field, you find people who've achieved it and do what they did. But Winston..."

"You said he was your *late* brother," Camila said softly. "I'm sorry."

This—the two seconds following those words—was when the next question would come. *How did he die?* Sure, most prefaced it with a do-you-mind-if-I-ask or something like it, but the question always came.

"I've lost people close to me too," she said in a whisper. "It's brutal."

James pulled his gaze off the glass, caught off guard by the flame that flared low in his belly. Here she was, surprising him again. It seemed that for each admirable trait he found in her, his insides sparked up some sort of response. And this—the tenderness he heard in Camila's voice, saw on her face—he admired it very much. Craved it, even.

"Yeah," he admitted. "It sure is."

They sat in silence for a moment more. He wondered then just who she'd lost in her life. Was it possible she'd lost a parent? The story about her grandparents said that could be the case.

"How long has it been?" she asked.

"Almost a year." He ran a thumb over the tabletop, back and forth, his eyes set on the motion. "I'm supposed to host some life celebration thing on his death date, but..."

At once Camila moved to a closer chair. Gently, she rested her hands over his, her touch soft as silk, and leveled a look at him.

That heat flared up once more as he met her gaze.

"It gets easier. Trust me, it does. And if you don't feel like hosting the celebration, don't. Tell your family you're not up to it. Let someone else do it."

"The thing is," he said, "even if someone else *did* host it, I don't think I'd show up for it."

"That's okay too." She'd said it as if it were some absolute statement. Like the grass is green or the sky is blue: it's okay if you don't go. But was it? And just how could she be so sure? *Okay* wasn't exactly a measurable thing.

A surprised chuckle sounded at his throat. "I'm sorry, I just…have never had anyone say something like that to me." An odd dose of relief washed over him, causing another small laugh to escape his lips.

Camila pulled her hands off of his and tucked a strand of hair behind one ear. "Like what?"

He shrugged. "Like…I don't know. I'm just used to people telling me to suck it up. Do what makes everyone comfortable." People like his mom and Zander. Adel in particular had told James to man up, throw the party, and rock out like Winston would have. The suggestion was insensitive at best, considering the lifestyle that eventually led to Winston's death, but James had let it slip.

Why couldn't he find a woman more like this? Sensitive, beautiful, passionate, and kind. That hot sting of fear sparked up once more. Exactly what was he doing? Looking for love from his personal chef?

It was one thing to force himself to do things he wouldn't naturally do. It was another thing to have it happen without his will or consent. James would lose control altogether if he didn't watch out. And that was one thing he could *not* let happen.

"Well," he said with a nod. "I've taken up enough of your time this morning." His chair scraped against the deck as he shot to a stand. His heart spiked out of rhythm in protest, an odd part of him yearning to stay by her side. It scared him even more.

He only hoped his face wasn't as flushed as it felt. "Please, enjoy the pool, the beach, whatever you'd like." He stepped around the table before adding to it. "I'll, um...take my lunch in my office again this afternoon."

There. The man he recognized was in there someplace. He lifted his shoulders as he stepped back into the house. To ensure he hadn't lost himself completely, James would attend to a few business matters when he got back to his room. He was already two steps into the home when he heard Camila's reply.

"All right, sir. I mean, Mr. Benton."

His shoulders fell.

Perhaps Duke's little assignment wasn't so harmless after all. They couldn't *all* live wild and free. James had been willing to hop on the train of spontaneity, as long as he could say where it went and when it stopped. But the pull he felt toward Camila— there was nothing intentional about it. Yet it was there all the same. And giving into it could spell disaster. James couldn't afford the risk. Not now, anyway.

No, James decided as he stepped back into the office. He'd save that behavior for Duke and get back to what he did best: work.

CHAPTER 8

*C*amila folded her arms over her chest and sighed as she took in the ocean view. Bright morning sunlight contrasted blues in the ocean and sky alike, creating a heavenly display.

The steady push and pull of the tides added to the bliss with sounds of serenity. And then there was that terrific ocean breeze, filled with mist and hints of salt that were—along with the humidity—causing the beach-type wave in her hair since she'd arrived.

Two days.

Two full days had passed since she and James Benton ate breakfast together on the patio. Which meant they'd almost been there a full week. Camila had been hesitant to join James that morning, worried he was asking her out of obligation. But he'd put that thought to rest with ease.

From what she could tell, James had taken a genuine interest in what transpired from Adel's careless post. The thought always led Camila to another musing: Adel Bordeaux *wasn't* his girlfriend.

Camila liked knowing that. Liked it a lot, actually. Perhaps he really was a decent guy. Discouragement crept in as she reflected on the shift in James' behavior. The way he'd darted out of his seat, hurried into the home, and requested his lunch in the office once more.

Part of her had been relieved at first; she needed time to digest the interaction they'd shared. But when he texted her that evening asking her to do the same thing with dinner, Camila worried she'd gone too far in comforting James over his brother's loss. She had felt a connection with him in those moments. A deep one.

Sure, she was relieved that her own story hadn't led to questions about who raised her and why. But beyond that, she'd been honored that he opened up to her the way he had. Perhaps though, after the fact, James regretted it. After all, it wasn't easy to appear broken in some way. And death—a loss like that—it had a way of breaking the best of them.

Yesterday, for the second day in a row, James requested his meals in his office. Even worse, he'd asked her to leave last night's dinner on the hallway cart for him to retrieve once he'd conducted his business. So much for presentation.

Today, she half expected to see his portion of the mansion roped off with a sign that read *Set the Meal Down and Back Away.*

"What do you think about our boss here, huh?" Gretta asked, breaking into her quiet musing.

Camila glanced over her shoulder to see the sweet woman polishing a side table beyond the open french doors. Gretta had told Camila a few fun facts about herself: She was from

Hungary (which was evident by her accent), she'd been house-keeping since her only child went off to college fifteen years ago, and she was enamored with actor Michael Douglas, and had been for years.

Camila set her mind back to the woman's question. "I think he's nice." Sure, it was sort of a kindergarten answer, but Camila hadn't exactly figured the guy out yet. At this rate, she never would. Which seemed to be his objective.

"He sure is a busy man, I'll tell you that much," Gretta said with a humph. "He barely spared a few words to say what he wanted done in the master suite. I had to practically pry him out of there to attend to it, as if there is not enough room in this villa or the entire beach for that matter. He stays put in that office all day long."

Camila grinned at the woman's candor. "How about you tell me how you really feel," she joked.

"How I feel is that if a man must work so steadily while on vacation in order to remain a billionaire, he shouldn't be a billionaire." She flung her arm in the air while walking to the other side of the table, her polishing cloth waving like a distress flag. "What else do you get all that money for if you can't take time to enjoy it, huh?"

"That's a good point," Camila said, but secretly she worried that James might overhear their conversation. He hadn't texted her yet this morning, and it was just twenty minutes until breakfast. Which meant he might finally crawl out of his hideaway.

On the menu today were freshly baked cinnamon rolls, Spanish-style eggs, and a fruit smoothie. In fact, it was time for her to put the rolls in the oven, she realized. "I'm making extra cinnamon rolls," she said to Gretta as she stepped through the open double doors. "Would you like one?"

"I'll say I would. Sadly, I'm on a cabbage soup diet for now. That means no sweets for me for six more days." Gretta gave an exhausted look heavenward and groaned. "I don't know why I torture myself so. In case I run into Michael Douglas, perhaps?"

Camila chuckled under her breath. "You never know. We are at the Royal Palm. Tell you what, if Mr. Benton enjoys the cinnamon rolls, I'll most likely make them again. You can have one then." She opened the pantry door, pulled one of her aprons off the hook, and looped it around her head.

"That sounds wonderful," Gretta said. The woman was quite pretty. Red hair with the slightest hints of gray streaked throughout. Her fair skin held very few wrinkles. That, combined with her sharp wit and sarcasm, added a girlish quality.

Heat poured over Camila's face while she slid the tray of cinnamon rolls onto the rack. As she closed the oven door, the spicy sweet aroma toyed with her senses.

"Good morning, ladies." A voice came from behind. James' voice.

"Good morning, sir. Mr. Benton," came Gretta.

An odd dose of excitement shot through Camila's chest as she spun to face him. "Good morning!" The enthusiasm coating the words made her blush. *Tone it down, Camila. The guy's been dodging you like the plague for two days straight.*

"Would you like your breakfast on the patio this morning? Or you could sit at the dining table of course, or the breakfast nook in the rear..."

"How about right here?" he asked, motioning to a barstool at the kitchen island before her. He slid one of the stools away from the counter before she could form an answer, not that it'd be anything but yes. It was *his* mansion for the month; he could eat where he wanted.

Even if it *was* likely designed for staff to sit down and have a meal away from the resort guests. Even if it *was* her main workspace and she'd be hovered over it attending to meal prep while he ate.

"I'm off to clean the master suite while I can," Gretta hollered, an edge on the words.

"Very well," James called back. He turned to face Camila once more. "I don't think she likes me."

Camila's face went hot. "I don't think she...*doesn't* like you. She's just very down to business."

Hints of a wry smile pulled at the corner of his mouth. "I don't mind," he said. "She's a hard worker. That's what's important."

"Right," Camila agreed with a nod.

"Oh, is that the beet stuff?" Though he'd just settled into the stool, James pushed away from the bar.

"Yeah," Camila said, lifting her eyes from the cutting board.

He strode right to the countertop where the three quarts stood and snatched one of the jars. He studied the deep purple contents before looking up at her. "Does it have to sit out like this for a while?"

Camila nodded. "Yes. It's ready now, though. In fact, I plan to serve it with lunch. Pulled pork sandwiches, red potato salad, and fresh peas."

"I can't wait." The slightest hint of a smile pulled at one side of his lips. The sight made Camila's heart stop, skip, and then speed into double rhythm.

If Camila could regain control of her body she would reply, but it was too busy having a response of its own. The heart-racing was only the half of it. Her cheeks were flushed, her brain was mushy, and a ripple of goosebumps had spread up her arms.

All from an innocent half-smile, Camila? Come on.

But if the way to a man's heart really was with food, the way to Camila's heart was appreciation for the food she made. She always had sucked up food compliments like air. They fed her creativity, her ambition, and her very soul.

"You don't mind if I have like, a little taste right now, do you?" James hadn't abandoned the jar yet, she realized.

"Not at all." She glanced down at her berry stained hands; one still held a massive strawberry while the other steadied the knife. "Let me rinse up and get you a fork."

"No, no," James said. "Just tell me where they are. I'll grab it."

"Ah..." While balancing fruit over the open blender, Camila took a step back and glanced at the drawer she stood in front of. "It's this one right here."

James raised a dark eyebrow as he looked down at the knob. He kept his grip on the jar and hurried over, careful as he tugged it open. His arm brushed against her apron as he reached in and pulled out a fork. He stepped away from her then, but not before Camila could breathe in the heavenly scent of him. Spicy, masculine. Camila wasn't one to use the word *sexy*, but his scent forced it into her mental rolodex in a blink.

He didn't return to his seat. Instead, James turned his back to the counter and leaned against it as he twisted the lid. Camila finished cutting the large berry in half and plopped it into the blender. Yet as she reached for the kiwi she planned to add next, she couldn't help but watch as James poked inside the jar.

"You're sure it's ready?" he asked. "You don't have to do anything special to it?"

Camila shook her head. "Not anymore, no. Go ahead and taste it."

James sank the prongs into the mixture, pulled out a heaping forkful, and ate it. A groan sounded at his throat as he closed his eyes and chewed. "Mmm."

Camila's grin widened, the elation swelling to the point she gave into a quiet giggle.

His face turned serious as he set his gaze back on her once more. "Marry me." The two short words were followed by a smile so spectacular that her breath hitched. It wasn't one of those formal grins, the ones stemmed from obligation or awkwardness. It was the sort of smile he might give to a good friend over an inside joke.

James Benton might have been holding a jar of beet kraut in his hand, but it may as well have been Camila's heart in that moment.

He chuckled low in his throat. "Seriously," he said as he screwed the lid back into place. "That is incredible."

Camila forced herself to pick up the kiwi. Inwardly, she willed the heat to leave her cheeks before they burst into flame. "I'm glad you like it." Okay, so it was an understatement. Camila was *thrilled* over how much he liked it. And if she were honest, quite affected by the whole marry me comment.

He rested his forearms on the counter and glanced around

the kitchen a bit. "Maybe I'll take in the view before breakfast. We've got another fifteen minutes or so, right?"

"Right," Camila said while glancing at the clock.

Without another word, James strode out of the kitchen and toward the double doors.

Camila set her eyes back on the kiwi. She'd removed the skin and was ready to cut it in half and add it to the blender with the power greens, yogurt, and the rest of the fresh fruit. Yet as she hit the blend button, her eyes focused on the action, she admitted that the scene before her might be a good example of what was happening on her insides about now.

James Benton was unpredictable. And absolutely gorgeous when he smiled. Her heart thumped out of rhythm once more. She forced herself to look at the bigger picture: either the guy had been giving her the brushoff for the last two days, or he'd legitimately had a whole lot of work to do. He was a billionaire after all.

Of course, another option lingered in her mind. One she couldn't get herself to ignore: He was in a state of mourning over his brother's death. It made sense, with the year mark approaching. Her heart ached at the mere idea. She wouldn't beat herself up for comforting him, she decided. She'd done the right thing, and that was final.

Still, before pushing her mind to other matters, Camila allowed herself to replay the interaction once more. James shooting her that lingering look as he sampled the kraut, the shocking words 'marry me' in the sound of his voice, and that full, knowing smile that crossed his face.

Goosebumps raced up her arms in the replay alone. As much as she hated admitting it, hope was starting to bloom. But hope for what—a good referral? A decent work relationship? A possible friendship as the weeks passed? It would be unrealistic to hope for more than that. Which was fine—she wasn't the least bit interested in anything more.

An irritating voice spoke up in her mind, one she hadn't been able to stifle in time. *Sure, Camila. Friendship. Just keep telling yourself that.*

ॐ

Marry me? Had he lost his mind?

James raked a hand through his hair and groaned. What in the name of all things holy had caused those two words to come out of his mouth?

This is why he should have just kept taking his meals in his office. *This* was why spending a month at the Royal Palms might not be such a good idea.

He took the stairs off the deck in a mad dash, pulled the phone from his pocket and, since Stephanie had forwarded all of his contacts to him so he could conduct business over the last two days, tapped the number for the man who'd come up with the dumb plan in the first place.

James squinted against the morning brightness as he shuffled around the pool and toward the trail leading to the beach.

"This is Duke," came his brother's voice.

"Hey," James grumbled. "I don't think I can do this."

"James? Why are you calling me from some random number?"

"I left my cell with my PA. Listen, I..." He almost didn't say what he wanted to say, but desperation got the best of him.

Anger too. Heck, this was all Duke's idea. "I asked my personal chef to marry me just now."

"Whoa, whoa, whoa. You did *what?*"

"Not literally, for crying out loud. I just...took a bite of this stuff she makes and looked into her brown eyes and said, '*marry me*' like some lovesick puppy."

A group of seagulls circled overhead, their cawing suspiciously close to the sounds of laughter.

"*That's* what you're freaking out over? That's called flirting, James. Sheesh. Welcome to the game."

"Well, I'm definitely not supposed to be flirting with the personal chef. No dating someone in the service industry, right? I'm sure of all the rules you go around breaking, that's *one* you stand firm on."

"You're wrong there," Duke mumbled, "but personal chefs don't really count. They're entrepreneurs, in a way. If you think she's hot, and you wouldn't normally let yourself go for her, then do it."

James glanced a pleading look heavenward, cursing himself for taking advice from his wild brother in the first place. And that's when he saw it. A red tailed hawk flying overhead. He followed its flight for a breath, watching the impressive wingspan of its matching shadow on the sand below. Something stirred within him, anxious energy in the pit of his stomach.

Twice since Winston's death, James had spotted such a hawk. His late brother had a firm belief that the hawks were there to send messages from the spirit world. To sort of lead the living into new paths. And while James had never embraced the idea himself, he couldn't help but think Winston was somehow trying to speak to him.

He shook off the notion and forced his mind back to the argument at hand. "I got kind of close to one of my housekeepers," James started. "Not like flirting or anything, she was in her mid thirties, I'd guess...but just friendly, you know. I'd ask about her family, where she'd come from, did she have any kids. Next thing you know I'm paying off her mother's mortgage because she was diagnosed with stage four cancer and had too many expenses to juggle it all."

"That's just you being a nice guy," Duke said. "Nothing wrong with that."

James' jaw tightened as a new dose of resentment flared through him. "A few months down the road I helped out with her ex-boyfriend's truck payment, her little sister's small business...heck, I even bought this woman a new car because hers kept breaking down between jobs and leaving her stranded on the roadside."

He shook his head, unwilling to admit that the incident with his old housekeeper was far from isolated. James had already learned this lesson the hard way. Helping someone out was one thing. Being taken advantage of was another.

"I've had the same driver for five years—his name's Leonard. I don't know if the guy's married or if he's got any kids. I don't know where he lives or what team he roots for. That's why things work out with him."

Duke groaned on the other end of the line. "Dude, you're overthinking this. Which is a very *James* thing to do, actually. You'd already know it if this chick was like that. You're not stupid."

James recalled a handful of lawsuits the Benton family had endured over the years. Ridiculous ones that were dismissed before they could even go to court most of the time. People often came up with get-rich schemes at their expense. But Camila might actually have good cause. She probably could've sued him and Adel both. Heck, she'd have a case for defamation of character. And she'd likely win, too, by demonstrating her loss of clientele after the dinner party.

But she hadn't done that.

He nodded while sucking in a dose of fresh, salt-misted air. Camila might not be wealthy like Adel or the other women he'd dated, but she wouldn't try taking advantage of him either. Perhaps he could do this after all. There was no guarantee for romance or anything, but James would be lying if he said there wasn't a spark there.

"Aren't I crossing some line if I hit on her at this point? She's, like, working for me."

"Listen," Duke said, "here's what matters: This personal chef of yours isn't a permanent employee. Heck, you can barely even *call* her an employee since she's independent, right?"

His shoulders lifted a bit. "True."

"Plus," Duke continued, "*I'm* the one who made the reservation in the first place. The resort found her for me, and you happened to step into my place. This chick's not going home with you. She won't be hitting you up for gas money on behalf of her crazy Uncle Joe. So just flirt like a normal guy, will you? Have some fun. Heaven knows that's what *I* had in mind when I booked the place."

James let Duke's words sink in. He was right. Camila wasn't some employee he'd brought on for the foreseeable future.

"Do you think I should address that and get it out of the way?" James asked. "I could say like, I don't know, that I'm interested in getting to know her and I don't want her to think of me as her boss."

This earned another groan from Duke, along with a few colorful words. "Come on, James. Think about how awkward that would be." He sighed. "I've got to get back to work. Just start flirting with her, will you? See if she's into it. Don't make it all weird by talking about it first. Women hate that."

"Fine," James grumbled before ending the call. But he wasn't so sure Duke was right. The last thing James wanted was for Camila to worry about the pressures of not disappointing her new boss, even if it was temporary. She wouldn't want to lose her job, and she definitely wouldn't want to lose the good word he planned to put in for her, so she might feel…obligated to entertain him in that way.

Equally bad was the fact that she might think he was using his position as a way to get what he wanted.

He glanced back to the sky, hoping to spot the hawk once more. No. Just some white, puffy clouds and a flock of seagulls in the distance. *Flirt like a normal guy, will you? Have some fun.* James could picture Winston speaking those very same words. Perhaps, in a way, he had.

"I'll try," he said under his breath. And with that, James selected every name in his phone, save Stephanie, Duke, and Camila's, and hit delete. Time to do what he'd come for—it was time to make better use of his time there.

Just as his determination took root, James spun to see a black town car parked along the circular drive on the other side of the property. And what was this? Camila stood beside it, talking to some guy in a suit. A driver, perhaps? He certainly wasn't gray-haired like Leonard. James could tell even from a distance that the man was young. And he was standing a little too close to Camila for his liking.

James shielded his face from the brightness as Camila tipped her head back in laughter and rested a hand on his arm. A sting of jealousy rushed through him, and suddenly he was tugging his phone from his pocket once more. Who knew if Camila even had her phone on her? He'd find out.

With quick fingers, he tapped out a text.

James: *is everything okay over there?*

He hit send before he could rethink it and watched. A bout of satisfaction struck as she pulled her phone from her apron pocket and looked at it. She shielded her face in a similar fashion, looking his way. At last Camila nodded, then set her attention to her phone.

At once a text popped up on his screen.

Camila: *Do you know anything about a yacht excursion for two?*

James: *Nope.* But then he recalled what Duke had said. *Heaven knows I planned on having a good time...* Apparently he did —yacht excursion and all. James watched the two talking in the distance, noted the flirtatious way Camila stepped closer and swatted a teasing hand toward the guy.

It was a new side of her, one James hadn't seen until that moment; she'd always been so...businesslike with him. He could fix that, couldn't he? He considered the trip once more, then tapped out an additional reply.

James: *Duke must have booked the trip, but it'd be a shame to let it go to waste. Would you be up for trying the yacht life with me?*

His pulse pushed fast and hard as he hit send. Each pump of his heart causing a tight ache in his chest, shoulders, and neck. He stared across the beach floor, beyond the side of the villa and its ivory statues and potted plants, watching for Camila's response.

She turned her gaze on him, and his quickened pulse raced hotter still. She spoke a few words to the driver before attending to her phone once more. The words *please say that driver's not part of the yacht crew* ran through James' mind as he waited.

And then it came.

Camila: *Why not?*

Triumph raced through him as a smile pulled at his lips. He'd been looking for a way to break beyond the professional layer, and call him crazy, but this seemed like the perfect way to do it.

A bout of nervous energy wrestled through him. This was definitely new territory, no doubt about it, but James couldn't get himself to worry about that any longer.

Despite the fact that he'd steered clear of choices like this, despite the fact that pursuing Camila Lopez made him more nervous than asking a girl out for the very first time, James was willing to risk it. If his instincts about her were correct, she might just be worth that risk.

CHAPTER 9

*I*t took Camila great effort to keep her irrational brain from coming to irrational conclusions. The moment she'd seen James' text, her heart had fluttered out of beat while her face went fire hot, and there was no way Kyler hadn't noticed.

It was as if James Benton had asked her to come along as his *date*, not his private chef who'd be preparing his meals for him on the yacht. Kyler had been ready to drive them to the excursion when he arrived, but James had asked for an hour to get packed up and ready.

Camila stirred the frosting for the rolls and sighed. She assumed the excursion was more of a ride-until-evening type of event. Maybe catch the sunset on the way back, but she was second-guessing that idea. As it was, James was checking in with his brother—the one who'd booked the yacht trip—to see what they could expect.

She eyed the rolls on the cooling rack, realizing she should attend to other things while they cooled. But what other things? She'd already given James his smoothie so he could start on it while he packed. But what did packing look like for her? Just how many meals would she need to prepare for? And what else should she bring?

If she brought a swimsuit it would be too assumptive; she was an employee, not a guest. But if she—

"I just checked in with Duke," James said, entering the kitchen with a small travel bag looped over his shoulder. "It's three days and two nights, so pack a few clothes." He glanced down at the cinnamon rolls and grinned. "Oh, can we bring these?"

"Yes. I mean, I'm planning on it. I just..." Camila drifted off as she tried to wrap her head around what he'd said. "Did you say *three* whole days?"

James nodded. "Is that okay?"

It felt as if a construction crew had taken up residence in her chest. Hammering away while building a new creation. It was just that, it felt very much like he was asking her out on a date of sorts. *You're cooking for him, you dork. Get over yourself.*

Suddenly James' brow furrowed. "You don't get motion sickness, do you? I'm sure they have stuff for that on board if you do."

"No," she assured. "I've been on plenty of boats. I should be fine." But she couldn't get over the idea of packing up meal items for the next three days. "I'll hurry and get some food packed up for the meals. I assume they have a full kitchen?"

"Oh," James said, a hint of laughter in his voice. "No, they'll have a cook there. An entire crew, in fact. Food, room service, all of that. Just bring yourself, some clothes, and a swimsuit."

Holy smokes. So she wouldn't be cooking for him. Now it really felt like a date.

"Of course," James was saying, "we can't leave these babies behind either." He motioned to the cinnamon rolls once more. "Mind if I steal one of these before we go?"

"They're not frosted yet," she said, assuming that would stop him, but it didn't. He grabbed onto the edge of one, tore a portion away from the roll, and brought it to his mouth.

"Mmm," he mumbled while he chewed. He grinned at her and readied to take another bite. "Taste good without it."

Camila gave into a grin, liking that the playful side of him had returned. Plus, there was the fact that he'd actually asked her to come along as his guest.

"I'm glad you like it," she said. It came out delayed, but she hadn't quite caught up. She pointed toward the doorway, hoping her feet would carry her in that direction even though they felt tingly suddenly. "I'll go get packed."

She paused for a blink as she noticed James looking at the pantry slip she'd just filled out. Was he checking to see if she'd ordered enough watermelon? Probably.

"Do you always sign your name like this?" he asked.

It was such an off question that Camila had to repeat it in her mind before forming an answer. "Like what?" She resisted the urge to walk over and take a look at it. She'd been signing her name the same way, heart dotting the 'I' since she was thirteen.

"With this heart. It took me a minute to realize that was part of your signature," James continued with a shrug. "It looks nice."

"Thanks. And yeah, that's how I always do it." She stood

there nodding until James set his attention to a sight out the window. She took that as her cue.

While hurrying toward the main spiral staircase, a very important detail shot to her mind: She wouldn't be working on the yacht. The thought nearly made her stop in her tracks. A bit of panic kicked in. This was a bad idea. What if he tried digging into her past? And why would he have her come along if she wouldn't be making his meals like she'd been hired to do?

He'd told her that he didn't want the trip to go to waste. And that his brother had paid for two. She nodded as that fact settled over her.

Relax, Camila. He's just being nice. She could do this.

She'd go along for the ride, bring a few good books, and just stay out of the way. When their three days was up, she'd go back to cooking for him and all would go back to normal. But that left one question even still. Which normal would they go back to? The kind where James spoke to her, invited her to eat with him, and joked about marrying her while tasting the beet kraut? Or the norm of him taking his meals in the office and not giving her a second glance?

Camila had no idea which it would be, but one thing was sure—she was anxious to find out.

Camila tucked her last few items into the dresser drawer and slid it closed. She took a step back to eye the walk-in closet. She hadn't expected to find such posh conditions, even if it *was* a yacht. Further, she hadn't expected James to insist she take the master suite. He assured her that he wouldn't take the room either way, and that she would get more use out of the extras it came with; a night and day bathroom, as well as the walk-in closet and generous ocean view. Besides, the other option was a room directly across from James with the use of a shared bathroom.

This seemed like the safer bet.

Camila walked back through the marble-floored bathroom and up the five-step staircase to take in the suite's view once more. Since they hadn't left the port just yet, an impressive array of boats bobbed alongside the boardwalk. Many boasted names like *Playin' Hard,* or the one she spotted three boats down called *Cheri Baby.*

The particular yacht they were on had a name of its own —*The Midnight Express.* A mysterious name, really. One that had her imagining what it might be like to lounge on the deck with James in the midnight hour.

Camila could hardly believe the way such thoughts crept into her mind. She barely knew the guy. Beyond that, James Benton had been—in her mind—closer to enemy than friend just days ago.

But there was something about him that made her want to see what else he had to offer. The fact that he'd made billions in his life—that alone said he was smart, savvy, and, she dared say, even powerful. Money went a long way, after all. But that only made the other sides of him all the more interesting. Every normal thing he did made her swoon. Pumping iron in the villa's gym. Snatching a cinnamon roll off the hot pan and eating it right in front of her. Not to mention the way he'd opened up to her at breakfast.

Her heart still twirled each time she thought of it. It seemed as if he wanted to get to know her, before he'd shut himself in the office for two days. And now this...

She shook her head, stepped over to the mirror, and tucked a strand of hair behind one ear. She'd opted for a sleeveless button-up blouse with a pair of navy high-waist shorts. The cream colored top would keep her cool despite the heat; she liked that, but she also liked the way it complimented her skin tone.

Two small taps sounded behind her, pulling Camila from her musings. She spun around to see James standing in the doorway. Dressed in a pair of charcoal gray shorts and a black V-neck shirt, he looked cover-ready for a spread in GQ magazine. His blue eyes locked on hers, and a dose of heat stirred around her still-whirling heart.

"We're about to take off. Would you like to come upstairs and watch as we pull away?"

She nodded, charmed by the idea. "I'd love that." Camila followed him to the main level where a set of winding steps led them up to the top deck. The one with the open bough. They headed to the front of the boat and watched as crew members unfastened the buoys. She'd met a few upon entering the yacht. Ethan, the one with the man bun, was the captain's son. And Karson with the impressive tattoos—he was Ethan's best friend. She guessed they were close to Kyler's age, just barely into their twenties.

"Would you two like to toast the occasion?" a woman asked from behind. It was Jill, the crew's chef. Camila had met her earlier as well. She stood beside a wet bar, two tall glasses in hand.

"Sure," James answered. "Thank you."

Warmth filled Camila's cheeks at his response, but she tried very hard to ignore it.

The yacht was a new model, the crew had told them that much, but even still the boat creaked and groaned as it pushed its way into new depths, free from the harbor.

Camila couldn't help but feel that a similar thing was happening inside of her. She was stepping away from her job as James Benton's personal chef and joining him on one of the finest yachts as his personal *guest*. A platonic one, but a guest all the same.

Still, a growing part of her assured Camila that things might not be so *platonic* after all. She knew chemistry when she felt it. And if James was up for exploring what lay between them—and only time would tell—then she could be open to it as well.

Don't fool yourself, Camila. You'll never let him get close to you.

"Here you are," Jill said, distracting her from the doubts in her head. Jill handed a half-filled glass to Camila and James in turn. She motioned to the tray resting on the nearby cocktail table where the bottle rested. "Help yourself if you'd like some more. I'll give you two some privacy." And then she was gone.

James lifted a dark brow once they were alone. "Privacy?" he said in a sinister tone. "Trust me, I didn't ask her to do that."

Camila laughed, anxious to prove the doubts in her head wrong. "I know," she assured, "but *I* did." She couldn't help but giggle as his eyes went wide.

"Well, well…" He drifted off there, his face softening as he lifted his glass. "To the both of us relaxing for the next few days, and enjoying…whatever it was my brother planned and is now missing out on."

That earned another giggle. A relieved one. She could do this. And if she wanted to let James in, she would. "Cheers."

"Cheers." James gave her a nod before tipping back his glass. He leaned a bent arm along the railing and looked out over the water. "I'm hoping we can talk about something," he said, setting his eyes back on her.

The construction crew was back, clanking inside of her chest as she nodded. What if he'd already discovered it? Maybe Adel had found out and called him or something. "Okay."

"I like the way you challenged me when you first arrived. Right away, it set you apart from a lot of people I encounter. Showed that you don't…gage the way you treat someone based on their status, I guess you'd say."

She had no idea where he was going with this, but another nod would at least show that she was listening. So she managed one that hopefully didn't look as anxious as she felt inside.

"Plus, I'm not exactly your boss in this situation. I mean, it's not like you're my secretary or PA or anything. " He shrugged and turned his gaze back to the glistening ocean once more.

Camila tried to pull her eyes off his face and do the same, but it took effort; his piercing blue eyes and chiseled jaw, combined with the mystery of the one and only James Benton, created one powerful pull. But at last, she managed.

"The truth is, I'm intrigued by you." He'd set his focus back on her, she could see it in her periphery. Feel it by the warmth of his gaze. She gulped, willed herself to set her eyes back on him. There was no stopping that heat that shot into her cheeks. Or the pounding of her heart as he elaborated.

"I considered not saying anything, since I don't want to make this awkward for you. And if you're not interested, I'll give you your space and, of course, put a good word out about your services as a personal chef. But if you're open to it, I'd like to get to know you, on a personal level, during our time here."

Camila was a pretty reserved woman when it came to gushing over a guy. At least, she thought she was. But the uninhibited thrill that shot through her at his words said otherwise. It was her turn to talk, but she was too busy keeping her swooning heart in check to even think.

Say something, Camila!

"I..." She nodded like a fool while searching for the right words. "I would like that," she said.

That was enough. She shouldn't add anything to it. So why was another assurance about to stumble off her tongue? "I'm definitely interested in that too."

An inward groan cried out. *Shut up, Camila.* But the smile on James' face said he liked hearing it.

"Great." And with that, he lifted his glass once more. "To getting to know each other better."

Camila lifted her glass, clanked it against his, and vowed to keep her wayward fears silent during her trip. She lifted her drink, then paused before taking another sip. "Cheers."

CHAPTER 10

*J*ames blew out a pursed breath as he eyed the watercraft before him. Paddleboats, canoes, and surfboards too. He glanced up to the deckhands. "This is what Duke had on the agenda?"

The captain's son, Ethan spoke up first. "Yep. We've got this, and a few other watercrafts onboard."

He motioned to Karson, who was walking toward the side of the yacht. He stopped beside a small compartment James hadn't realized was there. With a few taps to the keypad, a retracting door slid open to reveal an entirely different sort of watercraft.

"Jet skis?" James asked with a grin.

"Wave runners," Karson said. "Even better since you can fit two on one."

"That *is* even better," James agreed. "Let's just take one of them out for now then." He glanced behind his shoulder to see if Camila had made it down there yet. "She doesn't have to know there are two, right?"

Ethan chuckled. "I'm sure she'd want to share even if she did."

"So long as you're willing to let her drive," Karson added. "Women might not like to steer the ship when they get a chance, but they seem to want to take charge on these babies."

"Go ahead and grab Ms. Lopez," Ethan said. "We'll have this ready for you guys to hit the waves."

At the mere mention, James' pulse rushed. He thanked the deckhands and headed toward the swim deck, wondering if she'd gotten lost trying to find it. Yet just as he glanced up the short flight of steps to the upper deck, Camila appeared at the top.

Hair pulled back in a sleek ponytail, cheeks flushed the most gorgeous shade of pink, and baby browns set directly on him. He let his eyes wander over the swimsuit she wore, but warned himself to not let his gaze linger. A red one piece hugged her in all the right places.

"You um…ready?" The rev of an engine sounded, and James felt a similar thing happening low in his belly. That hum of anticipation like a force all its own.

"I think so," she said with a nod. Suddenly her hand went to her throat, her fingers toying with the gold necklace she wore. "Oh, do you think this will come off in the water? I probably should have removed it."

"That's a good idea," James said as she came down the steps. "Here, why don't you spin around and I'll unlatch it for you?"

Sure, he'd seen this on movies more times than he could count, but James wasn't about to let the opportunity pass. Camila turned her back to him. He reached up, looped a hand around her silky looking ponytail, and draped it over the front of her shoulder.

James breathed in that tangy sweet scent of her as he reached for the tiny latch. The tips of his fingers grazed her neck as he worked to secure the latch, but the appearance of goosebumps forming along her arms said she might not mind.

It took him a moment to unfasten the clasp, with as delicate as it was, but at last he managed. "There you go. Want me to take this to your room for you?"

"I can do that," Jill offered, hurrying down the steps. "I'll rest this in the box on the dresser, Miss." She took the necklace from James with a grin. "Go have fun on the water, then be ready for a delicious lunch on the beach once you're through."

"Thank you," Camila said. "That sounds wonderful."

Yes, it did.

"I can't get over the fact that I won't be the one cooking," she added as they headed to the side of the boat.

James gave her a grin. "It's going to be a nice change, I hope. Having someone cook for you?" He'd ended it like a question since he wasn't so sure that she *would* like it.

"Definitely," she said.

A relieved sigh pushed through his lips. "Good. Now let's go catch some waves."

It didn't take long to slip into lifejackets and hop onto the wave runner. The guys had been right about Camila wanting to take charge in the driving department. When James had offered, he assumed she'd shyly tell him he could drive first and, after a little encouragement, take the water reins. But that wasn't the case.

Sitting behind Camila while she took control didn't feel like the manliest thing, but he was dying to see what her style would be. Slow and cautious didn't seem like her cup of tea.

James adjusted his grip on the handles at the back of the seat.

"You ready back there?" Camila called over her shoulder. The life jackets they wore were the latest makes. Sleek and slender, not puffy and large. He was glad. It allowed him to get even closer.

"I'm ready," he hollered over the sound of the idling engine.

"Aren't you supposed to hold onto me?" she asked.

He liked and disliked that idea all at the same time. Sure he wanted to be close, but he'd rather have Camila hold onto him as he helped her lean into one sharp turn after the next.

"I've got these handles back here. I think they should keep me in place."

Camila shrugged. "If you say so. Hold on tight." With that, the engine revved and the wave runner kicked into gear. The back part of the craft was lower, with James weighing more than Camila as he did, but as the thing shot into action, it lowered even more.

James had been warned, but he hadn't exactly braced himself for the action. He'd never sat on the back while someone else drove. If he had, he might have known that Camila was right. Holding onto her would have been much better. He straightened his arms behind him, tightening his grip, and realized just how unstable his position really was. The slightest turn was all it would take to throw him right off the craft.

He'd barely recognized how dire the problem was when

Camila turned the handlebars hard to the right. The front end hovered there for a blink, but the back end spun with a vengeance, swinging fast and hard. He contemplated, for a split-second, grasping onto the only thing that might keep him from going overboard—Camila. But the force of his weight would likely yank her off along with him.

Soon the momentum reached its peak, flinging him right off the craft.

A massive splash.

One hard swoosh, and James was plunged into a barreling wave. He broke through the surface with a few of Duke's choice words, then bobbed with the rise and fall as Camila spun back around for him.

He covered another curse as it came to his lips. It took a second to recognize the sound he heard coming from her direction as she neared. She was laughing. Not just a shy giggle either. This was a hearty, full on, I just-dumped-you-on-your-butt laugh.

He joined in, enjoying the sound of it all too much. Liking the way she continued to surprise him.

"You okay?" she asked through laughter still.

He brought a hand up to the back of his neck and groaned. "I think I broke something."

Her face went serious, those brown eyes growing wide and worried. "Really? What? Not your neck..." she said frantically, gaze falling his grip.

He nodded. "Actually, I think I broke my...my ego." He held up his finger and thumb to show a tiny measurement. "Just a little."

Camila rolled her eyes. "Well, you probably needed that

then." Water drops glistened on her skin as she squinted against the sun, an unrepentant expression on her face. Dang, she was gorgeous.

"This isn't your way of saying you want to drive, is it?" She gunned the watercraft in two shorts spurts, bringing it close enough for him to climb back up.

James smeared water from his face and reached for the running board. "No," he promised. "It's my way of saying that I probably should have held onto you, like you said."

He grunted as he climbed back up and straddled the seat once more. He couldn't exactly wrap his arms around her waist and chance grazing…parts that he shouldn't. But there might be a solution. He glanced down at the curve of her hips and gulped.

"Let's see if this works a little better," he mumbled. Slowly then, tentatively, James cupped his hands around Camila's hips. He tried not to get distracted by the feel of her, warm beneath his palms. Leaning forward then, he lifted his chin over her shoulder and whispered close to her ear. "Be gentle with me."

Camila released a dark chuckle. "We'll see about that." She was teasing, of course. They both were. But as more heat brewed low in his belly—a result of her teasing—James mused that warming up to the baking beauty was a dangerous thing. His attraction for her was growing faster than the watercraft's wicked speed, and well he knew it could end with a crash and burn. Yet even still, James didn't want to get off the ride.

CHAPTER 11

*C*amila took in the layout before her, impressed with Jill's talent for beach picnic presentation. A thick, blue and white striped canvas kept the nautical theme, while the pair of legless beach chairs would allow them to lounge just inches off the ground. Even better, they'd be seated just inches from one another.

"Towel?" James said, gaining her attention from behind.

She glanced over her shoulder. Just beside the flag indicating their beach spot, a small stand held a stack of beach towels. Beyond that, rolling waves crashed into the ocean floor —a span of white, sparkling sand.

She shifted her gaze to arguably the best-looking attraction there as he lifted a towel toward her. Camila took in the glorious sight. He'd removed his life jacket already, and she couldn't help but be distracted by the muscular planes of his contoured chest.

"Thanks." The single word came out softly, almost shyly,

although they'd gotten quite comfortable with one another in the last few hours.

"Those were some crazy waves out there," she said while dabbing her cheeks with the towel. She tugged the hairband from her hair next, sent the length of it draping over her shoulders, and used the plush beach towel to sop up the moisture.

That full, genuine smile crossed his lips. "Yeah. You could say that."

She laughed as she caught hints of accusation on his tone. The truth was, as choppy as the water had been in parts, James was a very good driver. Of course, Camila wasn't convinced she'd been so horrible herself, but the fact that James had gone flying off the watercraft said otherwise.

"You know, I'm starting to think that you fell off that thing on purpose," she accused.

He'd been running the towel over his dark hair, but he stopped short and shot her a look. His eyes widened. "Really?" It was hard to hide her amusement as his brow furrowed. He looked baffled.

"It made me look like a bad driver right off the bat," she explained.

His face softened as it registered, and suddenly he was stepping toward her. "Actually, it made *me* look like a wuss for not holding onto you in the first place."

"A wuss?" The use of the word surprised her. "Why didn't you?"

A playful look blazed in his blue eyes. "Maybe I worried I couldn't keep my hands to myself." He glanced down at her hips before setting those eyes back on hers. Fire-hot heat stormed through her chest as he held her gaze.

This is dangerous.

Or rather, *James* was dangerous.

"So what do we have over here?" he asked as he motioned to the picnic. He walked over to the spread, letting his arm graze hers ever so lightly.

Forget the fact that she'd had her arms wrapped around him on the wave runner for the last hour, the contact still caused a dose of goosebumps to spread over her arms in a ripple.

Camila joined him beside the blanket. "Mmm. Cheese, bread, fruit…"

"No," James said, "say it like you do when *you're* the one who makes it. You know, with heart."

"Okay," Camila said with a grin. She cleared her throat, preparing to use the low, smoky tone of her voice. "Well, Mr. Benton, we've got a selection of fine cheese, everything from smoked Gouda to Swiss. Next we have a basket of herb-seasoned ciabatta bread, savory kalamata olives, and a cluster of fresh, candy-sweet grapes."

"And *champagne*," James added, nodding to the brass ice bucket in the shade.

"And our finest bottle of sparkling white wine, sir."

He tipped his head. "James."

"James," she corrected.

He nodded and puffed his chest. "I like how you do that."

"Thanks. This does look amazing. I'm actually pretty hungry after hanging on for dear life all that time."

"Yeah, but you were hanging onto *me*, so you liked it, right?"

"Maybe," she winked at him when she said it, and reveled in the fresh smile that transformed his handsome face. Her breath hitched.

The moment was surreal, if Camila let herself think about it. Here she was, about to sit back and eat lunch on the beach with James Benton, a guy she loathed just a few days ago. Even more, she was on a date with the man. And she liked it. She wasn't sure which detail surprised her most.

The paddleboards and canoes waited along the shore side— one end tucked into the sand, the other bobbing in the crystal blue water—courtesy of the crew from the Midnight Express. She figured that, after lunch, they could explore the water on those next.

As Camila settled into the beach chair, she discovered an array of meats and mustards to go with their meal. And there, propped on a tiny stand nearby, stood a copper pot filled with stunning white flowers. But not just any flower. "These are Camellias," she said, a smile crossing her lips. She leaned in to inhale the familiar scent and sighed.

"My grandma used to grow these in honor of my mother, since they were her favorite flower. In fact, Grandma used to say they made a mistake in the flower's name. They were supposed to be called Camila, like me." She didn't finish that line aloud, but Camila could almost hear Grandma doing it for her ...*because you're so beautiful, my sweet Camila.*

A sudden longing came over her. A desire to see her sweet grandma. Toss her arms around the woman's fragile frame and pull her in for a long embrace.

James looked over the flowers thoughtfully. "They really are beautiful. And unique. I don't know that I've seen flowers like that before."

In her mind's eye, Camila blew her grandma a kiss. At least she was in good company up in the clouds. She pushed past the emotion and set her attention back to the food. It was meant to be enjoyed, after all. And with the wide selection spread before them, an idea was coming to mind. "You know what we should do?"

"What's that?" James asked as he reached for the champagne.

"Let's make little bite-sized samples for each other. Pick whatever meat, cheese, and mustard we want, and let the other one try it. We'll see which ones we like best."

"You're on," James said. "But I've got to warn you. I'm going to be better at this than you think."

She lifted a brow. "Oh yeah?"

He shook his head now. "No. But I'll give it my best."

Camila was first to stack a creation of her own while James closed his eyes. After she fed it to him, James had one thing to say. "Why don't we have you do all of them?" He moaned and grinned. "So good."

He played along though, creating a small sandwich of his own. This time Camila spoke up after trying it. "The grape was an interesting choice," she said. "Maybe this was a bad idea."

James' eyes widened. "I'll do better next time. In fact, I think I'll use a thin slice of baby cheddar cheese with a salty, crisp cracker, and the delicious mustard with all the spice…"

The two broke into laughter.

"Baby cheddar?" Camila asked through a grin. "How could I resist that?"

They spent the next hour preparing samples for one another to taste and rate. He got better as the game went on, but he continued to sneak hints of fruit into his creations.

"Okay," he mumbled. "This is the last one. It's almost ready."

Camila kept her gaze on a distant palm tree as a breeze blew in, adding a slightly cool contrast to the wonderful warmth of the sun.

"This one is going to be amazing," he promised. "I'm seriously going all out."

Camila couldn't help but laugh. "It's not going to have a surprise grape in there again, is it?"

"Hey, I sampled that one before you tasted it. I thought it was good."

She shook her head. "I should probably be scared right now."

"Why? Because you have to taste my latest creation?"

"No, because I'm cooking for a guy with such messed up taste buds."

It was quiet for a beat, and suddenly she felt the warmth of him at her back. Her breath hitched as James moved even closer to rest his chin on her shoulder. The short scruff from his five o'clock shadow tickled her skin.

Slowly then, as if he knew the sensations it stirred in her, James moved up the curve of her neck, his touch teasing her every inch of the way.

"I've been looking at you all day," he said in that deep voice of his. "And I'd have to say I actually have very *good* taste."

A thrill shot through her. The sound of his words, coupled with the teasing warmth of his breath at her earlobe, it threatened to unravel her completely. At once, she pictured spinning around, looping her arms around his neck, and pulling him in for a glorious kiss right there on the beach.

Perhaps she really could do this. She could let him in, be in a relationship, and keep fear from getting in the way.

Just as that assurance ran through her mind, James brought his mouth to her neck, grazing her skin ever so softly.

So good.

She closed her eyes and tuned into the full press of his lips at the curve of her neck. Another wave of bliss washed through her as he repeated the action, causing the effects to rush over her in succession, like the tide washing over the shore.

She considered the events leading up to this moment: The hours they'd spent on the wave runner, being playful, teasing, and having fun. Their explosive interaction when she'd first arrived at the villa. The daydreams she'd had about cozying up to him in the hot tub. She reminded herself that this was, in fact, the very man who'd wandered into the pantry at Shimwah's party and made her heart beat out of rhythm. The man who'd opened up to her about his brother's loss.

Every detail made the taste of romance all the sweeter.

With his mouth still dangerously close to her ear, James let out a low groan, the sound resonating through her before he pulled away. "Okay," he said. "I almost forgot about your sample here. The masterpiece is complete. You may turn around now and try it."

Still in a near-paralyzed state of bliss, Camila let her eyes flutter open. She cleared her throat, then turned to see the concoction he'd put together this time.

There was no bread in this one; instead, a long toothpick bound pieces of meat, cheese, and olives alike. He had the morsels crammed so tight it reminded her of Grandpa's over-stuffed file cabinet, where—try as she might—Camila couldn't remove just one folder. The surrounding files always upheaving in the process.

"That looks…interesting."

A low chuckle rumbled in his throat. "See? I'm good at this too." The breeze caught his dark, wavy hair then, sending a piece to topple over his brow.

"Yes," she agreed, he *was* good—at thinning the differences between them. At making her want him more than she'd wanted any man before. There *was* chemistry between them. And Camila was ready to explore it. He'd opened the gates with his affections, kissing her neck from behind. She could give him a little in return.

She reached up then, secured the wayward strand between her fingers, and moved it back to blend with the rest of his hair. And what a fabulous head of hair it was.

Before she knew it, Camila was weaving her hand through the length of it, up and over his scalp, tasseling the damp strands as they fell over her fingers. It felt more intimate than she'd imagined, and the truth of it caused an entirely new thrill to pulse through her.

She lifted her hand, and then repeated the action, the tips of her fingers pressing gently along the way.

James closed his eyes, and a low, raspy sigh sounded somewhere in his throat.

She didn't want this closeness to end. Not yet. So she let her hand rest at the back of his head, began toying with the short, tiny baby hairs at the nape of his neck. He was so attractive. That strong jaw, squared nose, and handsome brow.

He opened his eyes, roping her in even further with that brooding expression. If there was any reservation left, a sliver of doubt about giving into the pull, it withered in the heat of his gaze.

His eyes narrowed as he leaned in, closing the gap between them. He must have dropped the sample he held because suddenly his palm was sliding softly around the curve of her neck.

More goosebumps.

Another dose of heart-pounding, beat-skipping excitement.

He glanced down at her lips, and Camila exhaled a jagged breath. She couldn't help but look at his in return, wondering what it would feel like to have that perfectly shaped mouth on hers.

Slowly then, James traced his fingers in the softest trail down her throat. He leaned closer still, gently, until his heated breath tickled her lips.

Yes. Please.

Her eyes fluttered closed as a rush of heat pounded through her chest.

At last he came in, pressing a very soft, very encouraging kiss to her lips. *Mmm. So good.*

He came in again, teasing, testing, making sure she'd accept his affections.

She would. *Absolutely.*

But suddenly, rather than bringing his lips back to hers, James pulled back instead. A cool breeze rushed into his place.

Camila opened her eyes to inspect him.

"Sorry," he whispered with a grin. "I couldn't stop myself."

Stop himself? Camila gulped, nodded, and tucked a flyaway piece of hair behind her ear. "No problem," she managed. *No problem? Ugh.*

Embarrassed heat filled her face as she tried to dissect the encounter. He'd barely even kissed her. And then he'd apologized for it? Talk about confusing.

As they finished their meal and moved on to the paddleboards, Camila mused on the encounter some more. Maybe he worried that he'd crossed the line or acted too soon. If that were the case, Camila would look for her chance to assure him that she'd wanted that kiss just as badly as he had.

Maybe they were moving too quickly. In the real world, Camila rarely kissed a guy before the second or third date. But this didn't seem like the real world. This experience, whatever it was, would end in a set amount of days. And for a reason she couldn't explain, she didn't feel like wasting a whole lot of time.

I couldn't stop myself, he'd said.

Camila lifted the paddle, thrust it back into the water, and grunted beneath a hefty stroke. Next time, she'd prefer he didn't try stopping himself at all.

CHAPTER 12

Candlelight illuminated Camila's gorgeous face as they waited for their fifth and final dinner course on the yacht's deck. The dimple in her cheek had been a rare sighting at first. But over the last two days, it'd been a near-constant attraction.

Their second day on the yacht had been a success. In some ways, James had enjoyed it more than the first.

They'd spent more time exploring today—this time a costal kayaking trip to some nearby cliffs, where they hiked up the mountainside and jumped into the waves below. Talk about a rush.

But as action-packed as the last two days had been, nothing stood out to him more than the moments they'd shared during yesterday's picnic. The temptation of her silky neck, the taste of her heavenly lips…His pulse raced just thinking about it.

In retrospect, he was torn over his decision to slow things down. Ninety percent of the time, James was glad he hadn't tried to take things further, as tempting as it had been. It was probably best to establish more of a friendship first.

And then there was that small but loud part of him that wished he could go back in time and make that moment really count.

But there was no going back, and that was for the best. Now, after another perfect day together, James felt confident exploring their chemistry. He only hoped Camila did too.

"And now for your fifth and final course," Jill said as she approached the table. "Dessert."

Before heading out to the cliffs that morning, the two had given Jill their preference for dessert. The woman rested the one he ordered—a chocolate mousse—in front of James. Camila had opted for the berry tart.

"There you are," the woman said, snatching the tray off the table's edge. "Enjoy, you two."

"Thank you," he and Camila said in unison.

The evening was a perfect seventy-four degrees, according to the digital thermostats placed throughout the yacht. And here on the deck, with the distant sunset stretching its color onto the waves, there couldn't be a better moment to share with the fascinating woman across from him.

Camila inspected her own dessert before looking across the table at his. "They both look delicious," she said.

Her brown eyes soaked up the colors of the sunset, reflecting an array of rich, warm tones as she inspected the dishes.

"So when someone else does the cooking," James said under his breath, "is there a part of you that's scrutinizing their work?

Like, *I would have cooked the asparagus longer,* or *taken the meat off the grill sooner?*"

She tore her gaze from the tart. "Sometimes," she admitted. "But that's not what I'm doing now. I usually pay attention to the things I like, and the things I don't like. I make note of what I could do to improve the overall experience, from the food to the setting. I'd say it's less scrutinizing and more…studying. I like learning ways to improve. Offer a better experience."

James nodded as he considered that. "I think we have a lot in common that way," he said. "It'd be easy for me to decide I know *enough,* right? I've done well with what I was given, but that doesn't mean I couldn't have done better. I always watch the investments I make; business and stocks I put money into. But you know what else I follow?"

She shook her head. "What?"

"The ones I *don't.* I make a habit of following the options I didn't pick to see if I made the right choice."

"That makes sense." Camila lifted her glass to her lips, but paused before taking a sip. "So here's a question for you. Do you beat yourself up about the ones you missed? I'd probably lose a whole lot of sleep over that."

James chuckled, recalling specific times he'd done that very thing. "I did at first. In fact, it almost stopped me from doing it. Duke—the one who booked this trip—he's more like Winston was. They never wanted to know if a deal they passed up made it big. But see, that's what I think makes me more like you. I want to know, not so I can beat myself up, but so I can make better choices next time."

Camila set her glass back down, lifted her gaze back to him. "Hmm. That's interesting."

James wanted to somehow bottle the moment. He couldn't exactly explain the vibration skittering over his skin as he looked at her. The living, growing connection that made itself known in every interaction they had. Assuring him that he and Camila *weren't* so different after all.

"Should we test out these desserts?" Camila said, pulling his mind from his musings. She dangled a fork over her triple berry tart.

"I think that sounds like a good idea," James agreed, snatching his spoon off the table. "Guess we can call this a study session then, right? It's almost part of your job."

She giggled. "Right."

James motioned to his dish. "Shall we?"

"We shall."

He sunk the tip of his spoon into the small dessert and got himself a nice spoonful. Camila did the same with her tart.

The rich, chocolate flavor, smooth on his tongue, nearly melted in his mouth. He'd definitely made the right choice.

"Well," she urged. "What do you think?"

"I think I chose right," he said with a grin.

"Oh, but how can you be sure? Remember, you've got to test out the one you *didn't* pick, just to be sure."

That. It was things like that witty comment that fanned his longing for her—the one low in his belly.

"You're right," he said with a grin. It was more than some raw desire for a beautiful woman. It was an appreciation for *who* Camila really was. A picture of what he never knew he could find.

"You try mine first," she suggested, readying a bite for him.

She lifted it to her mouth and blew. "It's pretty hot though," she explained. "Kind of burned my lip."

"Occupational hazard?" he guessed.

She nodded. "Always." She lifted the forkful toward him, and James leaned in to meet her partway.

The tangy flavor was delicious, tart and sweet all at once—like her. "Mmmm," he moaned as he chewed. And the crust. It was a perfect, savory compliment.

"Well?" The look on her face, coupled with the expectant tilt of her head, said she already knew the answer.

James dabbed his lower lip with the napkin. "I chose wrong."

Camila laughed along with him once he said it. "Let's see if I think so now," Camila said.

"Right." James prepared a nice spoonful of his layered desert and fed it to her across the table. He watched her expression after she ate it, curious to discover which she liked best.

She nodded, pointed a finger at him, and then dabbed her lips before speaking. "That was amazing."

When she ended it there, James started to guess where she was going next. "But…" he urged.

She shrugged and reached for her glass. "But you chose wrong." That sparked another round of laughter. Camila surprised him then by slipping the spoon from his fingers and sliding her fork in its place. She caught the edge of the mousse dish with the tip of the spoon and proceeded to drag it closer to her.

"We're trading," he realized as she brought another spoonful of his dessert to her mouth. Camila only nodded and moaned.

"Hey," he said, bringing the tart in front of him. "Did you

trick me just then?" Not that he minded. The tart was definitely his favorite between the two.

Camila shook her head. "Nope. You chose wrong, and so did I, since we both like each other's more."

"Ah." James tipped his head back. "This is opinion based. Of course." He took another bite, enjoying—just as much as he had the first time—the burst of tangy sweetness.

"You know what I liked most about that dish," he said, resting the fork onto the plate once he was done. He rested the linen napkin on the plate as well.

"What's that?" Camila asked.

"It reminds me of you. Sweet, of course, but with some sassy tartness to keep things interesting."

"Whoa," she said. "Spoken like a real foodie."

Camila rested her napkin over the dish and spoon with a nod. "Okay, well, I'll have to admit a similar thing then."

James liked where she was going already. At least, he thought he did. "How so?"

"I usually stay away from chocolate dishes. They're too... rich for my taste." She shot him a pointed look, and as playful as it was, James realized she was revealing something to him then. He leaned in, put his next breath on hold, and inwardly willed her to tell him more.

"This one was different," she continued. "Not as dense as I'm used to, but still dark and mysterious."

He tried to unravel what she'd said. "So basically, I'm not dense."

"Basically." Camila rested her hands on the armrests at either side of her, indicating she was ready to stand. But there was more James wanted to hear.

"Did you mean it," he asked, hurrying to his feet to pull her chair from the table. He offered his hand to her, and Camila took it.

"Mean what?" she asked.

James led her to the seating area along the open bough, wondering if he really wanted the answer to his question. Camila settled into the couch first, angling herself toward the center. He did the same.

"James?" Camila rested a hand on his leg, her expression growing concerned.

A battle warred in his mind. Did he want to dive into a topic that could, if nothing else, point to the ways they *didn't* match up?

"You don't normally date rich guys," he said. "Right?" He didn't like how it sounded aloud.

She nodded. "Um hmm. And I'm guessing you normally only date women like Adel. Is that because it's better for your image? To have someone famous at your side, I mean."

James shook his head, but as he considered the more accurate reason he dated women like Adel, he wished he'd have just nodded and agreed instead.

"So what, then? She seems to be more sour than sweet."

"Yeah, her personality is…not what I'm attracted to. But I've had to be careful over the years. All of us have. It's probably why none of us are married." He pulled his gaze off her and looked out over the water. It was getting darker now, harder to see much but reflections of light dancing randomly over the surface.

"My siblings and I—we don't want to fall for anyone who's more into our money than they are us."

"Oh." The single word came out in a hush. Like an afterthought. "Dating women with money helps you avoid gold diggers," she added.

James shrugged. "Maybe. Who knows?" When he met her gaze once more, he swore he spotted hurt in her eyes. Or maybe it was that guard she'd had up earlier, coming back into place.

He rested his hand on top of hers, toyed with the thin gold band she wore on her middle finger. "I'm not worried about that with you," he assured. "If you were someone out to get what she could from the billionaire she'd just started working for…" He squeezed her hand, chuckled under his breath. "You wouldn't have challenged me like you did when you arrived. I think, in some ways, it knocked down that barrier from the get-go. At least, for me."

She smiled. And just like that the guard was gone. The warmth he was growing very fond of returned. A softness in the set of her lids, the ease of her grin.

"I want to know more about you." It came out in a whisper.

That dimple sank into her cheek. "Where do you want to start?"

A hot thrill shot through him. It felt as if he'd just gained backstage access to his favorite band. He wanted to know it all. Everything, anything. Whatever she was willing to share.

Where did he want to start? That was a good question. James rested an arm along the back of the loveseat and squared a look at her. "Anywhere."

CHAPTER 13

*C*amila gulped as James' surprising reply echoed in her head. *Anywhere.*

She studied his handsome face, conflicted by the obvious interest he had in her. "Narrowing things down, aren't we?" she said with a laugh. She hoped it masked the odd dose of fear that gripped hold of her insides. A fear of him knowing about what lay in her past.

"Ah, I might hit the ladies room for a minute, if you don't mind." She shot to her feet, ready to make a run for the nearest restroom when a realization struck her. *Don't act crazy, Camila. You just need a second to breathe.*

She pointed a finger at him. "Don't go anywhere. I'll be right back."

She walked on then, the conversation playing through her head as she hurried through the doors and into the covered part of the boat. Her pulse sped up with her footsteps, fanning at the anxious flames in her chest.

I want to know more about you.

Where do you want to start?

Anywhere.

His reply showed just how interested he was in her. That he'd take whatever details he could get. Camila wanted to bask in that. To let herself feel flattered over the beauty of it.

But if they dove into any part of her life, save the very moment before them, it would surely lead to details she didn't want to give. Details she hadn't even told her best friend about.

As far as Gypsy was concerned, Camila's parents had been killed in a tragic accident. It was tragic, there was no doubt about it. But the cold killing of a human being was rarely deemed an accident.

Camila slid the pocket door closed, forcing the automatic lights to kick on. She fought to block off the headlines flashing into her mind. *Man Murders Wife Then Turns Gun on Self.*

Man. A brief scroll down the online article revealed the name of that man. Martin Lakes. Her mother, who'd taken on the name when they married, was listed as Isabella Lakes, but she'd gone by Izzy since she was little, according to Grandma and Grandpa.

If Camila tried hard enough, she could almost remember hearing the name on her father's lips. At least, she thought she could; it was hard to trust memories from so long ago. Especially since they'd been tainted once she discovered the truth.

Her mother had married an abusive man who eventually killed her. And her father? He'd been the killer. What if her mother resented Camila? What if Camila was the reason she'd stayed?

But there was more to it than that. If she'd worried she

might have her mother's bad taste in men, Camila had worried, too, about having a dad who was capable of what he'd done. Did that make her a monster too?

While she'd learned to accept that it didn't, Camila worried others would come to that conclusion. She could picture Adel's cruel post now.

Check out this article about @CamilaCooks' parents. Guess we're lucky she didn't kill James for running into her.

An explosion of fire-hot heat blasted throughout her body. "No way." She would *not* tell James what happened, and she wouldn't feel bad about it either. She would brush over it like she normally did and, if things got serious between them, maybe she'd tell him one day.

Camila amended the resolution in her mind. *Not maybe. Of course. Of course she'd tell him if the two were about to get married or something.*

Camila shoved her hands under the sink and ran some cool water over them. Rather than drying off with a fresh hand towel beside the sink, she patted her cheeks, forehead, and chin, allowing the cold moisture to calm the heat in her face.

She ignored the tightness in her shoulders and neck, forced out some pursed breaths, and took one last glance in the mirror. She could do this.

With that, Camila opened the door, headed down the hall, and stopped short as she spotted James at the head of it.

"I know I promised not to move, but I found the coolest seat in the house this morning, and I wanted to show it to you."

The excitement in his voice made her grin. And when he reached for her hand, slipped his fingers through hers, the tightness gripping her muscles melted away. A feeling of warmth and comfort took its place as James led her up the two sets of stairs until they reached the very top deck.

There, she followed him to the front of the ship where the metal railing came to a point.

"Is this the part where I climb onto the railing and you come up behind me and we feel like we're flying?" she asked.

"You're onto me," he said with a laugh. But then he pointed into the darkness at the ship's far edge. "Don't you see it?"

She squinted, unable to see beyond the light's reach. "See what?" But that's when it came into view. A grey, shadowy outline of something suspended beyond the edge. "What is that?"

"Haha," he chuckled. "This is going to be fun." He hurried over to a panel along the side of the boat, gave it a few taps, then rubbed his hands together. "Ethan and Karson showed me this. It's awesome."

Camila set her gaze back on the sight in time to see a set of lights flip on. "A hammock chair? Over the water?" And that's just what it was, too. She stared down at the gap between the railing and the hanging chair, realizing that the floor below it was made of glass. She could see the lights reflected there and in the glass railing surrounding the addition too.

James swung back part of that glass railing, allowing them to enter. "Madam," he said in a low voice.

A round of nerves rustled through her as she moved from the shiny wood floor of the deck, to the near invisible surface beneath the hammock. The chair was beautiful. An iron, gold case with intricate detail, like a birdcage that had been cut in two. In the rounded hollow, cushions of bright white seemed to hover like puffy clouds.

137

"This is incredible," she said. Now she understood the excitement she'd seen in him. It was like a dream.

James tugged a blanket from a nearby storage bench and wadded it beneath his arm before joining her. "Here," he said, tossing the blanket onto the seat and offering his hand.

He steadied the swing as she climbed in, and soon he was nudged up beside her, spreading the plush blanket over them both. It was warm and soft, a wonderful contrast to the crisp bite in the air. And when James cozied into her, infusing her with the scent of his spicy aftershave, Camila basked in the gift of having him near.

She reminded herself of what she was about to share, and a boost of confidence swept in; she could tell him about her life story, leave out the one dark detail, and focus on the rest. Besides, her therapist had drilled an important message into her mind: *"You're not defined by the events in your life, or even the people who gave you that life. What defines you is the way you live, love, and use the gift of every day."*

Never had she recognized the truth of those final words like she did right then. The endless ocean crashing beneath them. The warmth of him contrasting the delicious breeze. This moment was, indeed, a very beautiful gift, and Camila vowed inwardly to make it count.

"I went paragliding a few years ago in Italy," James said as she snuggled up to his shoulder.

She inhaled another deep, heavenly scent of him. "You did?"

"Yeah," he said with a laugh. "It was during one of our celebrations for my dad's life. Before Winston passed. He and I went to together. It was one of those seat type of deals, like a park swing, where you're suspended side-by-side beneath the parachute."

He chuckled once more and ran a hand over his face. "Winston was talking so much smack. Saying that I was going to freak out and scream like a girl. So we get moving, and I'm fine. I'm actually just enjoying the view and the wind and everything. Winston, he started off with a couple of hoots, and then he gets quiet. I figured he was just taking in the scenery like I was. So I said something like, *it's incredible, right?* He didn't answer so I tried again with a different one. *Can you believe this?* Still no answer.

"So I lean my head between the straps to look over at him, and the guy is passed out cold."

She gasped. "You're kidding."

James' laughter was contagious. "Serious."

"That is hilarious. Did you give him crap for it?"

"You know it. And since we were so close—like, best friends, really—we had a special pass to really razz each other. More than the average sibling."

Best friends? The words put a fresh take on the hurt he must be going through. "I didn't realize you two were so close." The sentence was coated in a sadness she hadn't meant to reveal. "That's a great memory," she added.

"Yeah," he agreed with a sigh. "It sure is. Have you ever been parasailing?"

"No, I haven't."

James turned toward her, that thoughtful furrow in his brow. "I saw a few people out there while I was running on the beach. Think the resort offers it. If they do, would you go with me when we get back?"

His question answered a concern Camila had noticed throughout the day. A worry that things would go back to normal once they got back to the villa. His invitation said that wasn't the case.

"Have you gone since that time with Winston?" she asked.

"No," he admitted.

Emotion struck her fast and hard. She couldn't exactly say why, only that she sensed it might help the healing process, something she inwardly longed to do. "Yes," she said. "I would love to."

He put his arm around her then, pressed a kiss to the side of her head. "Thank you."

She grinned at how natural that kiss felt. At how comfortable and close they'd become.

James spoke more about Winston and his family, giving her a glimpse into a life that seemed more normal than she might have guessed. They were close, and they enjoyed one another's company. She admired that as much as she envied it. Camila couldn't imagine having such a big family. Hearing about the adventures they shared over the years made her long for it.

He told her about the private plane crash that killed both his father and his grandfather close to five years ago. And how the grief was, at first, unbearable, especially for his Grandma Lo. But they'd come together, helped strengthen one another after the loss. Camila couldn't help but admire them.

Soon the conversation turned to stories in *her* past. Camila kept calm as she explained. "They died together in a tragic accident," she explained. "I was staying with my grandparents at the time. Luckily, I was already quite close to them. It just made sense that they'd be the ones to raise me."

James shook his head in stunned silence. "And your father's parents?"

"I never knew them," she said. "His father was never in the picture. His mom died when he was nineteen."

When she went on to tell him about the loss of her grandparents, Camila was touched by the tenderness in James' response.

"Man," he said, voice somber. "It's like burying two sets of parents."

"True," she agreed. "But it hadn't been the same as losing my parents at a young age. Grandma Lopez had been steadily declining for years before she died. And Gramps, while he enjoyed pretty decent physical health through his old age, he got diagnosed with heart failure a few months before he died.

"What I mean is, neither was taken suddenly or without warning, and I'm grateful for that."

"Wow," James said. "I've got a lot to learn from you."

Camila was resting her head on his shoulder, but she pulled away to look at him. "What do you mean?"

"I mean, you lost four of the closest people in your life— your whole family, from what it sounds like—and instead of being bitter and angry you...point out what you're grateful for?" He shifted in the seat until he faced her. "I'm serious, Camila. I want to be like you someday."

A rush of warmth circled her heart. She might be suspended from a hammock far above the waves, but James' comment lifted her higher still. She basked in the feelings of hope and happiness and potential, until a sliver of guilt crept in.

You didn't even trust him with the truth.

She shook it off. If he earned her trust, she'd tell him about it one day.

But would she? She hadn't even told Gypsy.

"The hardest part of not remembering much about my mom —both of my parents, actually—is that it's oddly easy to doubt their love for me. I worry that, since I don't have memories of them tucking me in at night, hugging me tight or tickling my toes...that none of those things ever happened." She shrugged. "I mentioned that to my Grandma once, and it really upset her. Enough that I didn't bring it up again."

"But she told you how much they loved you, right?" James prompted.

Camila gave him a nod. "Yes, of course. But what else would she say?"

James held her gaze. "Yeah, but how else would they have felt? Really, Camila. Parents...they love their kids. They just do."

She grinned, liking how easily the sentence came to him. He'd been loved well by his parents, and she was happy for him.

"You know," she said, shifting the focus back to him. "I think you're already doing pretty amazing things. I mean, you lost your brother and best friend a year ago, and you're still working hard, doing your best to move on." She drifted off there as James shook his head.

"Not really." He took Camila's hand, rested it palm up on his lap, and traced a finger over the lines and crevices of her palm. It felt good. Surprisingly so.

He traced up the length of her fingers one by one, seeming to gather his thoughts. Or maybe debating whether or not to share a particular detail.

She wouldn't blame him for holding back. Heaven knew she was.

With his gaze set on her hand, he spoke up at last. "I feel responsible for Winston's overdose."

The waves rushed and roared beneath them at his words, the response seeming to mimic the reaction in her heart. An urgency to correct him—to assure James that he wasn't.

But she knew, from experience, that he needed to be heard, understood. Not dismissed. "Why?" she asked.

His eyes clenched shut for a long blink before he answered. "My siblings don't know this. My mom doesn't either. But I really laid into him the night before he died. We'd all done what we could to help him over the years. Everything from giving him money to denying him money, to interventions he both accepted and declined at different times."

He lifted his gaze to her then, cupping her hand firmly. "I was fed up with him. I'd given him the chance to shadow a friend of mine, Tyler Lang. He's an entrepreneur in the architectural industry. Winston claimed he wanted to invest in his company, so I put myself out there for him, bought him a ticket to meet the guy at the Cincinnati airport. It would've been a great way for him to break into the industry as an investor. Not that he had a lot of his own money at that point, but we all agreed to help him out in that way, as long as he was doing something useful with the funds. Anyway, the best part about the job is that it would've gotten him away from LA and the temptations he faced there. Start new, you know?"

James nodded for a beat. "I really thought he was going to do it that time. Just...leave all the crud behind once and for all. He was starting to get clean too. Showing a lot of promise.

"But then, he texts me the night before he was set to leave— not even a phone call—but a text saying that he can't do it. To tell Tyler that he's sorry but he's not going to be there. I called him right up and laid into him hard. Told him a few choice things I'd been dying to say over the years. That he didn't have anyone but himself to blame for his misery. That he was throwing away a gift that could change his life."

James pressed a hand to his temple and sighed. "I was on a roll, so I just kept going. Told him it was his fault we weren't as close as we used to be." James sent her a look. "We'd drifted apart over the months leading up to his death. Then I told him that if he wasn't going to Cincinnati, he'd have to tell Tyler himself. I refused to do it for him. That was our last conversation."

Camila's heart dropped.

"He was discovered by his housekeeper the next morning. Since I was the last person who'd called him, she called me even before the police. I think she was in denial at first because she didn't believe he was really dead. I drove out there, saw him before the ambulance took him away. It was obvious." He shuddered, and Camila couldn't hold back any longer.

She leaned in, slipped her arms solidly around his chest, and pulled him in tight. "I'm so sorry," she breathed. A mean pain ripped through her as she imagined how hard it must have been. From dealing with his brother's addiction, feeling responsible for his recovery. Allowing himself to hope—after so much heartache—that he might finally change. And then waking up to that phone call. Seeing his brother. Witnessing, for himself, the gruesome grip drugs had on his life.

All of it brought on such a storm of emotion she could barely hold it in. "I can't imagine," she said in a whisper.

James pulled back to look at her, moisture glistening at the corners of his eyes. "This is what I mean," he said. "Most would agree that what you've been through is...far worse. I just want to heal already. Forgive myself, maybe. Or at least, *learn* what it was I did wrong." He rubbed a hand down his face. "And pray I never have to go through something like that again."

The words *what I did wrong* stood out like a sharp edge. She didn't like James taking the blame for his brother's actions. "We all go through life doing our best, and even still we make mistakes all the time. I'm sure you know this already, but let me just...make it clear, in case you don't. Winston was the only one who could save his life. It sounds like, to me, that you guys did all you could. The rest was up to him."

James dropped his hand from the side of his face. "Yeah, but what if he just would have made it past *that* night? What if he wouldn't have overdosed that night and shown up in Cincinnati instead? What if *I'm* the one that set him off and—drove him to—"

"Drove him to what?" Camila interrupted. "To making his own choice about how he'd deal with a brother who loved him? Wanted to help him? That's not your fault."

James held her gaze, his expression shifting to a near plea. Between the tension around his blue eyes and the tight set of his jaw, it seemed as if he were begging her to convince him she was right.

"I have his journal," he said. "I've had it since he died. It was on the coffee table, just a few feet away from where he'd..." He broke off there and shook his head.

"I know that if I go through it, I might find something about our conversation. That it's what drove him to his last reckless act. Or even if it doesn't, Winston might point a finger right at me in a bunch of other pages. Say, I don't know, it was *my* fault he ended up the way he did. He was sick of being compared to me. My mom compared the two of us a lot."

Camila let that sink in for moment, putting herself in his shoes as best she could. "So you haven't gone through it yet?"

James shook his head.

"If you're like me," she said, "things like that journal can really cripple you. It seems like it's holding some sort of power over you." She thought back on a tactic her grandmother always used on her. "Imagine that you read through it, and it's as bad as you can possibly imagine. He's blaming you, your family, whatever."

James nodded. "Okay."

"Now tell me this. What's worse: reading it once and for all and dealing with whatever's in there, or spending another month or even *year* worrying about what it might say? Right now, an inanimate object is holding you captive. Don't let it. Take the power back by reading it already."

His shoulders dropped a bit. A sigh fell from his lips. "You're right."

"Who knows," she added, "you may even find a few gems in there."

He nodded some more. "True." Quiet took over as he drew circles onto her other hand, a seemingly absent action. "We're going to be heading back to the villa tomorrow," he said after a while. "You can say no to this if you'd like, heaven knows I might, but would you go through it with me?"

A new gush of emotion flooded over her. Filling her with so much heat, both heavy and sweet, Camila felt she might cry. "Of course."

CHAPTER 14

*W*ell, that hadn't gone how he'd thought it might.

James shuffled into the restroom and splashed water on his face. Camila, who was waiting for him in the hammock swing upstairs, had surprised him yet again. He might not be anyone's pet, but James would eat out of her hand any day. Everything she offered was just so…good. It went far beyond the food she made.

Her words, her kindness, her wisdom.

Their emotional connection had grown deeper than he thought possible. The trouble was, he hadn't been planning to work on their emotional connection so much as their romantic connection. If they didn't kiss again soon, he might get pushed right into the friend zone.

Sure, he might have rushed things when he kissed her on the beach, but James needed to kiss those lips before another chance passed him by. He snatched his toothbrush from the drawer, piled on the paste, and gave himself a pep talk while he brushed. Three minutes later he was ready to go.

He moved through the yacht quickly, not wanting Camila to wait too long for him. But as he approached the hammock swing once more, the cage-like structure lighting her up like an angel, a bit of nerves crept in. Like walking-a-girl-to-the-door type of nerves. Or that spin-the-bottle type of tension tightening his chest as if he was back in middle school.

"Sorry about that," he said while settling back into the chair beside her.

Camila shrugged. "That's okay. I snuck in a quick little break too."

James caught hints of mint on her breath, and smiled. *Please say she's got the same thing in mind.*

But how on earth were they going to jump into this? Duke was right—James really *had* lost his mojo. Even still, he wasn't used to sitting down next to a woman one minute and trying to make out with her the very next. *Don't overthink it, James.*

"I'm really glad this yacht trip came up, and that you agreed to come along," he said. "I know that, at the Villa, I've been sort of hot and cold."

She lifted a brow, the smallest hint of a grin working onto her face. "Maybe a little."

Her candor sparked an honest explanation. One he hadn't planned on sharing. "That's because I was attracted to you. And I didn't want to be." His pulse spiked.

Camila's cheeks turned pink. "Hmm…And now?"

James' chest grew tight as he pulled in a breath. "I still am. More so, of course, since I've gotten to know you."

He realized there was more to say, mainly about his reluctance over those feelings. "I don't have reservations any more though. I think that, if we wanted to, we could actually have a relationship—a very good one. And I like that."

James studied her expression as his words hung in the air. Her brow lifted. Not the flirtatious lift over just one eye, but the even raise across her entire brow. She was surprised by what he'd shared.

A gulp sank past his tightened throat.

It took only a second for that expression to shift. The soft pull at one corner of her lips. The appearance of that dimple in her cheek. And suddenly, he was soaring with the evening birds on the wind.

She grinned. "I like that, too." Her gaze fell to his lips.

James could hardly believe the moment was real. This woman who was warming up to him had despised him just a few days ago. And now...

He leaned in, barely pausing to feel the heat of her breath, and pressed a kiss to her silky lips. Once, twice.

Her lips parted as he came in again—this time for a slow and lingering kiss.

So good.

Heat stirred low in his belly as he kissed her once more, settling into a pace of sweet succession. A push and pull like the tide. James could spend a lifetime here in this place, soaking in the sensation of her mouth on his. It was the closest thing to heaven he'd known.

Camila slipped her hand up the back of his head, fisting his hair along the way. It reminded him of their time at the beach, the alluring action that caused him to kiss her in the first place.

A thrill of triumph rushed through him. Later, he'd think

about the fact that he'd almost missed out on this. About how—had he not taken Duke's advice—he may have never seen Camila again. But for now, James would focus on the moment. It was, like she'd said, a gift, and he planned to enjoy it.

❧

Never had kissing felt like this before. James Benton was talented in many ways, but this—his ability to lure her under a spell with his masterful mouth—might be his greatest talent of all.

And his hands. The way his warm palms gently cradled her neck. Or wrapped solidly around her hips as he pulled her onto his lap. Camila knew the moment couldn't last forever, but in her memory it would. She'd never forget the effects of his kiss. Tender and teasing one moment, persuasive and urgent the next. And no matter the pace, fused with a passion she hadn't known.

She had to say goodnight and go back to her room, she knew that much, but ending such a moment was no easy feat. *A few more minutes,* she promised herself. *Then I'll say goodnight.*

A whimper fell from her lips as she gave into the passion once more, tipping her head to one side while his lips moved to her throat. He planted a trail of kisses down the curve of her neck, up and over her shoulder, his warm breath teasing her skin along the way.

"Camila," he mumbled just behind her ear. "I think we should say goodnight now." He planted a small kiss by her earlobe.

Her brows lifted. Part of the spell did too, allowing her to recognize what he was doing. Finding the will she hadn't yet summoned. "You're right," she said with a nod.

James hands circled her waist as he came in for another kiss, this one to her lips. Her thoughts went flying yet again. Why say goodnight when the going was *so* very good? A rush of that powerful euphoria came back with a vengeance.

That was why.

She couldn't let herself get carried away. And something told her, in their physical connection alone, that James could be very convincing if he wanted to be.

"Okay," she said between kisses. "Let's say goodnight now."

James pulled back to hold her gaze. His chest and shoulders swelling as he nodded. "Okay." His hands slid off of her hips slowly, reluctantly. "Goodnight." It came out in a whisper.

Camila gave him one last kiss, short and sweet, then forced herself to climb off the chair. She looked over her shoulder as she stepped back onto the deck. He held her gaze for a blink, the longing expression on his face fanning at the heat once more.

She grinned, half-tempted to go back and join him. Instead, she cleared her throat and summoned the word she didn't want to say. "Goodnight."

CHAPTER 15

*C*amila looked out over the water as they neared the harbor. Blue had always been one of her favorite colors. And this—the endless shades of ocean blue against the cloudless sky—was almost as hypnotizing as James' heavenly eyes.

It had been an incredible weekend, a dream, really. And last night? Just the recollection of their time on the hammock caused a rush of lingering bliss to roll through her. So why was it so quickly replaced with this odd degree of fear?

A quick glance over her shoulder said James was still on his phone. He'd been on it since lunch was through. Sure, he'd apologized for having to "step away and conduct a bit of business," but Camila couldn't help but worry. What she'd experienced last night was closer to a fairytale than anything she'd known. Which was great. Except that, well, gaining something so beautiful meant that you could lose it too.

It was an odd thing to admit, but Camila had, in some ways,

lost it all. The people dearest to her were gone. Something about that had lent her a sense of empowerment. *What could hurt me now?*

But today, Camila had an answer to that—found in the very man she was falling for, and fast. The acknowledgment opened two opposing floodgates: one welcomed all the flutters and feels of falling in love; the other let loose a rush of panic.

Camila sighed as she leaned onto the railing at the back of the boat. The sun spread warmth across her back like a blanket. From the time she was young, Camila felt a level of love from the sunrays. It was as if God himself was reaching down to say everything would be all right. That—despite how lonely she might feel—she was never really alone.

And while it lent her comfort in that moment too, Camila couldn't stop her mind from forging back into the treacherous territories of her off-the-wall dream last night.

It had all started with Adel. She'd popped into view, phone in hand while writing a slanderous social media post about her. "If Camila plans to follow her father's steps, she can simply change her page name from @CamilaCooks to @CamilaKills." She giggled at herself and hit *post.*

James wasn't far behind. He strolled in wearing a tux, his diamond crusted cufflinks bright and glistening.

He walked toward Camila, or so she'd thought until he veered over to Adel instead. One glance at her post, and he let loose a massive belly laugh. "Guess we're lucky she doesn't take after her father. She might have killed me for destroying her precious ostrich eggs."

The two burst into laughter.

A dream as it might have been, the fury that gripped Camila

was hot and hard to quench. She'd marched over to the pair and knocked the phone out of Adel's hand. "They were *quail* eggs, you idiot."

Adel threw back her head and cackled. "Like we care." The cruel woman narrowed her gaze, took a long step forward, and locked her flaming green eyes on her. "Did you actually think you were his type? After he dated someone like *me?*"

A shiver rocked through her at the recollection. That sentence, even if it *had* come straight out of her nightmare, hammered fear into Camila's heart even still.

The dream had ended with Adel and James in a fit of laughter. As if the idea that he could ever love her was no more than a joke.

The horror of it haunted Camila for the remainder of the day.

She hated feeling distracted while bidding farewell to the crew she'd become so fond of, but even in those brief goodbyes, and during the drive back to the villa as well, the worry wedged into her mind.

Part of her wondered if she should have simply opened up about her past. James liked her, he really did. But she hadn't presented *all* of her. He liked the side of her with the sad past and hopeful future. But would he like her once he discovered the darkness too? Would he worry it could taint their shot at a future?

Back at the villa, Camila unpacked her things, wandered back to the kitchen, and fastened an apron around her waist. It felt good to be back. The sunset's glow pouring in through the west windows. The colors reaching the opposite side of the house where they bobbed and swayed over the waves.

James had asked her to go over Winston's journal with him. Such a personal and intimate request. Would he follow through with it now that they were back? Or would the familiar setting of her working for him put them back on different levels?

She hated admitting it, but it seemed more likely that he'd go back to ignoring her. After being glued to his phone throughout most of the trip back, James had taken to his office, apologizing to her once more.

So what now? Would she get a text asking her to bring dinner to his office once again? Or worse yet, one saying that her services were no longer needed? That she could pack her bags and go home?

"Hey," he called, pulling her out of her musings in a blink. He stepped into the kitchen, a wide grin on his face. "I wanted to show you what I've been up to. It took a while, since I'm no good at social media. And I had to get my PA to help me, but look."

He tugged his phone from his pocket and tapped the screen. There, beneath his verified profile name and picture, was a posted review for Camila Cooks: *Five stars for this incredible private chef. Camila is as personable as she is professional, offering a wide selection of fine food with grace, class, and culinary precision.*

Camila's heart beat wildly out of rhythm as she read. She paused to glance up at James, still stunned that he'd done this for her.

"My PA had her writer friend help. But it was all my own thoughts, of course. She just...says it better."

She moved her eyes back down the screen and read on: *I highly recommend Camila and her services as a professional chef. Whether hosting an elegant dinner party or a romantic dinner for two, Camila will bring a zest for fun and food alike. I'll definitely hire her for jobs in the future.*

"You didn't have to do that," she said. "It's amazing. Thank you." He'd tagged her in the post. Or rather, whomever posted it for him had, which meant she could have a few new followers by now and maybe even some job offers.

"It's the least I can do after what happened." He tucked his phone back into his pocket and slid his arms around her. "I know we're not on the yacht anymore, but I still want this to be like a vacation for us. I could bring someone else in if you'd like. Let them do the cooking."

A grin spread over her face. Her insides broke into a happy dance. He wanted to keep spending time with her. That knowledge thrilled her as much as his post did. But as for the cooking… "I love to cook," she assured. "It doesn't feel like work to me. It feels more like play."

James pointed a finger at her. "That was good. I should have had *that* in the review."

Camila wrapped her arms around his back and rested her head on his chest. "Thank you, again, for doing that. It means so much to me."

"Haven't you figured it out yet?"

Camila pulled away just enough to meet his eye. A tiny part of her feared he might echo what Adel said in the dream. "What?" she asked.

"I'm kind of falling for you."

Those few words were like a sugar rush to her soul. She willed herself to believe it, fully, use it to push away her doubts. "I'm falling for you, too."

His phone beeped then, and James tugged it from his pocket

and looked down at the screen. Without even meaning to, Camila followed the action. She'd been just looking at the social media post with him, after all. But the bubble that popped up, just a portion of the actual text beside to his PA's name, caused her insides to plummet. But only because she could swear she saw her name in there just beneath it.

James tapped his thumb on the bubble and swiped, causing it to disappear.

He looked up at her then, his blue eyes guarded suddenly. "Excuse me for a moment." And with that, he strode out of the kitchen, leaving Camila to wonder just what his assistant had found.

CHAPTER 16

*J*ames couldn't get out of the kitchen fast enough.

He'd seen enough of the sample text to know Stephanie was sticking her head where it didn't belong. He swiped the screen to read the text as a whole.

Stephanie: Call me. I just found something on Camila that you're not going to like.

Angry heat climbed up the back of his neck. He was going to give Stephanie a piece of his mind. The nerve of her, digging into Camila's past like she was some kind of criminal. There was no missing her obvious lack of discretion. Stephanie knew better than to be so blatant; she knew he'd likely receive the text with Camila by his side.

Call me when you get a minute—*that* would have sufficed.

The heat burned through his chest as he typed out a return.

James: Stay out of it, Stephanie. If Camila has something to tell me, she will. You're crossing a line here. Step back.

A big part of him wanted to say more than that, but he

didn't. A stream of curses fell through his lips. The last thing he needed was Stephanie—a woman who seemed to have feelings for him as of late—planting doubt in his mind about Camila. Heck, it wasn't like he'd proposed to her or anything. And what could she have found out, really? Knowing Camila, it couldn't be anything big.

There he was, letting Stephanie get inside his head.

Stop it, James. Let it go.

The best way to do that was to get rid of his phone. He was tempted to step out onto the patio and hurl it into the turquoise pool below. He forced himself to walk it to his bedroom instead, deciding to tuck it next to the black journal for the time being. An inner voice said he was avoiding *two* things now —the sight of the items side-by-side said it all. But James rejected that idea.

He'd already decided to go through the journal with Camila, and he would. But he wanted a few more days to ready himself. He'd need to accept whatever it was he found in those pages, and that would take some mental preparation.

And the thing about Camila's past? If there was anything he needed to be aware of, James was sure she would tell him before their time at the villa was through. If Stephanie was developing feelings for him as he feared, she'd be coming from a biased perspective. He'd give Camila the benefit of the doubt.

A recollection came to mind then. Camila promised to go parasailing with him. He'd get that planned, see what else the resort had to offer, and put his energy into dating Camila during his time there. Still, James couldn't quite stop the doubt that boomed in the back of his mind. *Camila might be one investment he'd live to regret.*

CHAPTER 17

Camila sighed as she woke up to the bright sunlight, thoughts of James already drifting through her mind. After spending nearly three solid weeks with him, James Benton had become the last thing she thought about each night and the first of her thoughts every morning.

She snatched her phone off the bedside and eased into her new routine: looking through pictures she and James had captured during their adventures together.

The most recent shots had been taken after their final dance lesson with the one and only Christian Lopez. Talk about incredible. Camila had followed the child dance star since her youth, encouraged that someone with the same last name was making it big.

She never would've guessed she'd one day be taking dance courses by the star in a beach resort across the country.

She scrolled through the next few. James kneeled up to the sand creatures they'd made on the beach. Grains of sand clung to his skin as he put finishing touches on the seahorse. She posed beside the giant turtle in the next one, and then came Camila's favorite—the two leaning over their smiley starfish while James kissed her cheek. What couldn't be seen in the photo were the events leading up to that picture.

Camila had been hovered over the starfish, putting the finishing touches on its face, when James snuck an arm beneath the sand. She'd been so shocked to see the sand move on its own that she screamed. It wasn't until he poked his fingers up through the surface that she realized it was only James.

As the days had passed, he seemed to get more comfortable, playful, and affectionate too. She didn't have any pictures of their time in the hot tub, but nights spent soaking in the soothing warmth while the waves crashed against the nearby shore—those were something to look forward to all their own. Especially when they allowed themselves to give in to moments of passion.

The mere recollection put heat in her face and bliss in her heart. James was amazing, and even though they'd be leaving the Royal Palm in one week's time, Camila felt confident their relationship would continue to grow back in LA too.

But today was significant. Today was the day they'd go through Winston's journal. The timing seemed right. She and James had had their fun on the yacht, spent the two weeks that followed in a long running dating spree, trading one adventure for the next. Days relaxing and talking about life, family, and friends. Camila had grown closer to him than she thought possible, and she was ready to be a support for him too.

While getting ready for the day, Camila stayed very aware of what might be in store. Potential heartache and tears as James sifted through the entries in his brother's journal. She hoped there'd be plenty of good moments too. Memories and kind words that brought a smile to his face. Whatever they found in those pages, Camila prayed James would be freed from the trap of misplaced guilt and regret.

"How are you this morning?" Gretta asked Camila as she neared the kitchen.

"Wonderful," she said. "How about you?"

Gretta lifted the centerpiece from the dining table—a bowl of mixed apples—and dusted beneath it before setting it back in place. "Not as good as you, I can tell you that much." The woman gave her a wink and then fanned at her face. "Whatever's going on between you two has him acting like Mr. Wonderful. Ever since your yacht trip, he's happy and smiling and not moping around like an angry mobster."

Camila chuckled.

"You seem happier too," the woman accused. "Sitting there with a silly grin on your face while you cook. I tell you, love has a way of showing itself, and with you two—it's obvious." She gave her a pointed grin before disappearing into the hallway.

Camila had been wondering when Gretta would say something. The resort had assured James that whatever happened at The Royal Palm would remain private; they prided themselves on a strict policy where privacy was concerned. But James was realistic in his approach, saying that even if tabloids *did* catch wind of their relationship, he wouldn't mind. It'd only make it easier to pick up where they left off once their time at the villa was through.

Things like that made her heart melt every time. He was

serious about their growing relationship. Which was wonderful, because she was too.

"What's for breakfast?" James asked as he entered the kitchen, an act that often caused Camila to picture being married to him. Preparing a nice dinner as he came home from work while the kids played out back.

He came up behind her, rested his hands on her hips, and planted a kiss to her neck. "Mmm," he said with a moan. "This is pretty tasty. This spot right here."

Goosebumps rippled up her arms as he pressed another kiss to her delicate skin. A giggle slipped past her lips. "Umm...I can't remember what we're having. My mind is going a little fuzzy."

He chuckled under his breath. "Mine too. Hey, I've got to show you this great shot Marcus got of us on the beach."

She'd nearly forgotten about their surfing day. Marcus, the instructor, had been generous enough to snap a few shots while they were out on the waves. And another while they stood beside their propped boards. That's the one that popped up on his screen first. It was a great picture, too. James had one arm around Camila, the other propping his surfboard. She'd just been looking at pictures of them together moments ago; despite that, she could hardly believe her own eyes.

He was such a stunning man, there was no denying it. Rich and powerful too. But Camila had come to know the man he was inside. So when she looked into those deep blue eyes, took in the changing expressions on his handsome face, that's what she saw. A man she admired. A man she could trust. He'd put himself out there with the social media post, promoting her as he had, and already the interest was pouring in. From some big names, too.

"Oh, I like this one the best," she said as he swiped from one picture to the next. The two were seated on their surfboards side by side, and James had prompted her to lean in and give him a kiss, right there for all eyes to see. It was one thing for the resort staff to see them together; they were sworn under a contract. The guests, on the other hand, were not. But if James wasn't worried about word getting out, then neither was she.

"I think I do too," he said, leaning in for a kiss. Their lips had barely touched when his phone started to buzz. James pulled back with a groan. "It's probably Duke. I'll be right back."

Camila watched as he strode out of the kitchen, through the dining area, and right to the french doors. He pulled one open, stepped onto the patio, then closed it behind him.

A recollection came to her. One she'd forgotten until then. It'd been two weeks since their yacht trip came to an end. But on that day, when James was showing her the review he'd posted on social media, his personal assistant had sent him a message. One that, if she'd seen correctly, had mentioned her.

She'd written it off easily enough—heck, Stephanie was the one who'd just helped him post the review—but as she watched James pace the balcony, that furrow creasing his brow, anxious heat thrummed under her skin.

Whatever he was hearing from the other end, whatever he was saying in return, she could tell that it wasn't good.

A cool wind rushed over James' face as he shuffled to the edge of the deck, phone held to his ear. "Stephanie?"

"Please don't be angry. I just need you to listen."

"Is this about Camila?" he'd asked.

The pause in her response was an answer of its own. "You're dating her now," she said cautiously, "I know that. So I think you should be aware of a very disturbing part of her past. You might not want to be dating—"

"Her past? I know that she grew up without her parents."

"Yeah, but do you know why?"

Now it was James' silence giving him away. There was nothing scandalous about an accident. So was there more to the story? "Of course I know. And you can consider this your last warning, Stephanie. I asked you to leave her alone, so do it."

Ending the call didn't feel final enough. As he looked at the small phone in his hand, his arm ached with the urge to hurl the device into the open wind. Perhaps he should've left the thing back in the closet.

What was Stephanie so worried about? That Camila was some money-grabbing thief? That simply wasn't the case, and James was sure of it.

What if she'd lied about her parents' death? Perhaps they were still living, and in a bad way financially. Maybe they'd convinced her to seek him out and come up with some scheme to get their hands on some cash.

A sick knot rumbled through his gut at the thought. A betrayal like that would sting.

Perhaps he should come out and ask. Give Camila the chance to tell him if she hadn't been completely honest about her past. He didn't want to be some distrusting boyfriend, but...

The mere word *boyfriend* made him realize that he hadn't made that official with her just yet. He wanted to. But could he handle having a girlfriend when one call from his PA could send him into a full-on panic?

He didn't have an answer for that. Perhaps only time would tell. For now, James had his brother's journal to go through. The idea made his gut curl anew. As soon as breakfast was through, it'd be time to unzip that leather case and see what it held once and for all.

Talking about it with Camila, deciding that today would be the day—that had been one thing. But to think about how quickly that moment would come, how damaging the discoveries might be, was another.

With fear gripping hold of him once more, tightening his jaw, chest and throat, James shut his eyes and sent a few short words to the heavens. *Please, help me get through this. Help me heal. And...*An image of Camila floated through his mind. *Please let her be as incredible as I think she is.*

CHAPTER 18

*C*amila ran a brush through her hair while eyeing the vanity mirror. She smoothed a hand down the length, forced herself to set the hairbrush down, and squared a look at her reflection.

"Maybe I should just tell him," she mumbled. Camila didn't think James was entitled to know *everything* about her past. He wasn't. But did she really want him to find out some other way?

No. Already Camila had to fight off some paranoid frenzy each time Stephanie reached out.

Another part of her spoke up. A usually quiet corner of her heart. It said that, for now, James was in love with the Camila whose parents had died. That was *almost* the real her. But it still fell short. What she really wanted was someone to look at the real Camila, the one whose father murdered her mom, and to love her exactly the same.

That love would mean even more. And so would hers, because she'd trusted him enough to share such a vulnerable piece of herself. Of course, they hadn't used the L-word just yet, but she was definitely falling in love with James, and Camila was confident he felt the same.

She nodded and set her resolve. Yes. She could do it. Before their time at the resort was through. She straightened her blouse, smoothed a hand down her cutoff jeans, then walked through a quick squirt of cherry orchard body spray.

Ready.

The mansion was bright today, but not sunny. There was more of a luminescent glow pushing through the glass of every window. Camila could hardly keep her eyes off the view as she headed up the central staircase. The clouds created a cooler feel, the blue sky accented by purples and grays rather than the warm tones of bright yellow and gold. And though it was as lovely as it ever had been, signs of the impending storm caused an odd sense of foreboding. One Camila worked to shake off.

Earlier that week, she and James had explored the villa together. They'd discovered a bonus floor at the very top, a cozy loft with pitched ceilings, comfy lounge chairs, and a juke-box. That's where they'd planned to go through the journal.

Like James' room, the sitting area opened up into an adjoining area—a game room that they had yet to explore. Perhaps once James had done what he needed to do, learned what he needed to learn, they could dispel the lingering dark-ness with air hockey and indoor hoops.

Camila stepped onto the top floor at last, and spotted him at the entrance of the loft—a small foyer with a rug, a bench, and a potted plant. She took in his posture: Head bowed, shoulders curled, gaze set on the book in his hand. And suddenly all of her worries—the insecurities over James accepting her as she was—

all of it melted. This moment was for him. James had been putting this off for a solid year, torturing himself with what he might find. Time to put it behind him at last.

"Ready, Eddie?" she called.

James inhaled deeply, nodding as he strode toward her. "I think so." He took hold of her hand, his skin warm against hers, and brought it to his lips. "Thanks for doing this with me. If it weren't for you, I'd probably be putting this off for another year."

"I'm happy to do it," she assured him.

He slowed as they entered the room and nodded at the options around them. "What will it be? The lounge chair; we'll both have to squeeze into that one, the moon chair, the sofa, or the jumbo-sized beanbag?"

She imagined sitting beside James in each one before settling on what she thought would be best. "Let's do the bean-bag," she suggested.

"The beanbag it is."

It took a moment to get comfortable as the suede covered bag shifted beneath their weight, but soon they were nudged up together while the bag puffed up around them like a cocoon.

She dropped her eyes to the journal as James unzipped it. One side, over the corner, another side, another corner, all the way across the top. He pried open the front, causing an array of loose papers to scatter about with a swoosh. Most stayed within the confines of the open case, a few fluttered just beyond.

One scrap landed right on Camila's lap. A napkin with a sketch on it. "He was an artist," she said, pinning it between her fingers and thumb.

"Yep," James said, leaning in to inspect it with her. It resembled a character drawing. A man standing behind a bar holding a drink mixer over his shoulder with a double-sized grin on his face. Bulbous cheeks and a miniature forehead framed a set of kind eyes. He wore a nametag on his vest, *Stew.*

"This is from a bar he frequented," James explained, pointing to the small logo in the lower corner. *LA Brews.* Her eyes drifted to the penned words just above, a note from Winston.

Stew, Stew, he's our man. If he can't do it, no one can.

Camila grinned. "He liked him. He must've been kind to him."

"Most people liked Winston," James said, snatching another sketch from the heap. This was a thin tear-off notepad from an LA hotel. James lifted the top page to reveal blank pages beneath, and shook his head. "Let's see what this one's about," he said, flattening the page once more.

A woman with a sleek bob in a tiny dress. This one was also like a character sketch, but with a bit more accuracy than Stew's drawing. In one hand, she fanned an impressive display of dollar bills. An array of shopping bags hung in her grasp on the other side, taking up most of the small page. One bag boasted the words *she loves me.* While another bag, this one harder to make out due to the small print, read *she loves me not.*

An ache seeped into her chest. He had the same problem James did. It made sense, of course. But what a lonely feeling that would be. Not knowing if someone really loved you or if they just wanted your money.

Camila tipped her head to read what he'd written sideways along the length of the notepad: *Oh, Melanie. Why you gotta be like that?*

James blew out a *tsk* and set the small notepad to the side. "He knew how to pick them."

"Here," Camila offered. "I'll put the ones we looked at in a pile." It wasn't a generous offer or anything, but the look James gave her said otherwise. Or maybe it was just the acknowledgement that he wasn't alone in this. That he had someone to be there with him.

His lip turned up at one side. "Thank you." He gave her a quick kiss before moving on to the next one.

It was simple, really, but something about the action warmed Camila's heart. This was real. What she and James had was very real. She'd once read an article that talked of extreme circumstances or events and how they—good or bad— emotionally connect people.

She and James had shared several highs, with a log list of activities to show for it. But they'd opened up about their lows too, and were all the more connected because of it. That thought remained someplace in the back of her mind as they continued to sift through Winston's unique journal entries. She hadn't spotted it until James pointed it out, but each of those entries were dated someplace, usually in the shadows.

They weren't in any sort of order, which made the search for his final words more challenging. But the journey was an interesting one to say the least. He was witty, snarky, and keenly observant, evident in the details of his work.

As sad as it was, getting to know someone after they'd already passed, she felt a great amount of gratitude as well. She was getting to know someone very important to James, and that made them important to her as well.

Yet as their two piles shifted, the once-large stack of unseen pictures dwindling in size, a spark of concern grew in her mind. What if James was left without any answers at all? Or worse yet, what if his greatest fear came true? What if he discovered that his own brother—this sad but beautiful person who'd left this life behind—blamed James for all of his troubles?

CHAPTER 19

*J*ames watched a drape of dark, deep clouds creep across the horizon. Gone were the harmless white puffs he'd noticed earlier that day. In came a looming body of purple and ashy gray. The storm was heading straight for the beach, bringing with it sounds of distant thunder.

"It's going to be a big one," Camila said, seeming to follow his gaze.

James knew their lunch break was over, that he should get back to the journal and finish the job, but he wasn't ready just yet. Instead, he pushed his plate, empty save the sandwich crumbs and pickle wedge, to one side and reached an arm across the table. With his palm up, he wiggled his fingers expectantly.

Camila glanced down and smiled. She took hold of his hand, but shifted to a chair closer to him. The restless ocean and oncoming storm were at her back now.

To James, it was a picture of himself the day before that dreaded call came. Unaware of the approaching darkness that would change his life forever.

Camila rubbed a thumb over his hand. "You holding up alright?"

He managed a nod, though he wasn't so sure. "It's weird, but as we get to the bottom of that stack, there's an odd mix of emotions..." He shook his head. "In one sense, I'm relieved. Glad I'm not finding anything really ugly or pointed. But then there's another part of me that so badly wants *something*. Validation. Appreciation. I don't know, some sort of acknowledgement that I was really trying to help him out."

He sighed, working to calm the anxious knots clustered within him. "It's dumb."

"I don't think it is," Camila said. "I liked the one he drew of you guys at the family party. It gave me an idea of what family gatherings look like for the Bentons."

That it did. James favored that one as well. In fact, he'd set it aside with a few choice others. Winston had taken his time with that one. Captured most of the family gathered around the kitchen. Some sat to the bar, others stood alongside. It was at one of the celebration parties they held. Brazil, if James remembered correctly.

Somehow Mom had talked James into cutting this massive apple pie for everyone. He'd agreed, but boy had he made a mess of things. Winston's drawing featured mangled heaps on pie plates and jubilant smiles on every face. Betzy had her head tipped back in laughter, while Mom looked to be covering her grin with one hand. James half-expected his own expression to look miffed or humiliated, but it hadn't. Winston had given him the biggest smile of all. In that picture, James looked like someone who could laugh at his own mistakes. Was that how Winston saw him? Was it an accurate representation?

He wasn't sure. But he wanted it to be.

"Well," Camila said, giving his hand a squeeze as they came to a stand. "You ready to get back in there?"

"No," he blurted, but then a laugh snuck up his throat. Camila had picked up one of the plates, was reaching for the other, but at James' reply she set them down, scooted in closer, and wrapped her arms around him.

Her lips grazed his earlobe. "You're doing great," she said.

Goosebumps broke out over his skin in response to her touch. "Say that again," he urged.

She giggled, her warm breath triggering that wonderful heat in his belly. "You." She kissed him there before speaking again. "Are." Another kiss, this one longer. "Doing a great job," she breathed before kissing his neck once more.

He wasn't used to the tables being turned. He groaned as his hands caught her hips. "You're using my own tactic against me," he accused. "I like it." That was an understatement. James was pretty sure that Camila had singlehandedly managed to wipe every conscious thought from his brain with her touch alone.

He mused then, that there was nothing he wouldn't do for Camila. No wonder Winston had been willing to dish out the cash to keep Melanie around. If his feelings for her were anything like this, what James felt toward Camila, he'd probably do the same. Anything to keep her close.

The wayward thought caught James off guard. Why had he thought that? Camila wasn't anything like Melanie, which was *why* James was attracted to her in the first place. She didn't want any handouts. In fact, her pride wouldn't let her accept one even if it was offered.

He set his gaze back on Camila's pretty face. When her gorgeous brown eyes locked on his, heat shot through every limb all the way to his toes. It was time to let go of his doubts and trust this woman with everything that he had. Everything that he was. To tell her just how he felt.

Tenderly then, James cupped her cheek, softly running a thumb along her face, and dared himself to do it. "Camila." It came out in a raspy whisper. His pulse shot into overdrive as he considered the next few words he would speak. He pulled in a shaky breath and forced it out. "I'm falling in love with you."

That smile of hers, the closed-lip grin she often gave him, spread over her face as her cheeks burned a new shade of pink. "I'm falling in love with you, too."

Another explosion of heat pulsed through him. "Actually," he added, "I've been *falling* in love with you since the yacht trip." He nodded, gulped, and soaked up the sudden confidence rising within him. "I *am* in love with you."

Now her teeth were showing, that full and gorgeous grin that made his heart feel like it'd skipped a beat. "Good. Because I love you, too."

Complete.

That word floated to his mind as James moved in for a kiss. He relished the feel of her pretty mouth on his, the subtle but coaxing touch of her tongue, and the longing whimper that sounded in her throat.

He tightened his grip on her waist as she ran her hands through his hair. And while it caused that low belly heat to rev hotter than it had in years, James reveled in the fact that this was more than lust. This was love. And Camila felt it too.

The thought urged him to back Camila against the glass door and press against her as they kissed. He wanted nothing more than to celebrate—in a different way—the love that they'd found in one another.

He wanted her, but that didn't mean she was his to take.

James tried to tell himself that very thing as he slowed the kiss. The trouble was, Camila's touch became more sensual then. The lingering push and drawn-out pull of each heavenly kiss felt so good he nearly ached. He tilted his head, deepened the kiss with a moan before forcing himself to back off once more.

"I could kiss you all day," she said against his mouth.

Hearing that was a pleasure all its own. James grinned. "Me too." Forget the fact that only milliseconds prior, he'd lost all sense of self-control. But it was coming back now. "Should we head back up to the loft or...take this to the hot tub?" He was half-teasing, but the mere sound of that idea caused his defiant pulse to rev even more.

She giggled and gave his chest a slap. "The loft. We're almost done, you know."

He nodded and forced his mind back to their task for the day. That familiar clash of relief and disappointment warring within him once more. "Right. Let's get to it."

Her wide, innocent eyes held reflections of the impending storm in the distance. And for a reason he couldn't explain, a new sort of chill pushed through him.

⸎

It didn't take long to get back into the zone. The loft had taken on a life of its own after the hours they'd spent in there. And now, with the brightness beyond the surrounding glass replaced with evidence of the approaching storm, it seemed all the more fitting.

They were down to the final few entries, three dozen at most. And who knew what dates they'd come across with this batch?

So far the entries had reflected a time span within the last five years of his life, the most recent one dated a few weeks before his death. It was a self portrait reflecting the steps he'd taken toward sobriety in a tug of war. Him at the center and a rope at either side. The words *clean, sober, and free* were scrawled across the twine rope at his left. He leaned heavily toward that side in the depiction. But the rope tugging at his right, the words *my infinite vice* labeling the source of that pull, had a grip on him even still.

James mused over those words as he sank back into the beanbag. *Infinite vice?* Winston had given it so much power. There he was, in rehab when he'd written that entry about the battle he wanted so badly to beat.

"Look at this one," Camila said, holding out an entry with nothing but text. There'd been a few of those in the bunch, but not many. James leaned in to read it, aware that it could say the very things he dreaded finding. But as he took a closer look at the formation of words, the title along the top, he realized it was a poem.

Once

The steps in my path didn't feel like my own.
Once, a long time ago.
I fought for a freedom I hadn't known.
Relished my triumph while claiming my throne.
We danced and you felt like my very own.
Once, a long time ago.
I watched the man I used to know.
Drift from my body and take my soul.
No more a dance—YOU had control.
Once, a long time ago.
Every fiber aches to get me back.
The man I lost when I loosened my grasp.
Once, a long time ago.

An ache tore through James' chest as he read it once more. He found a date, written upside down along the bottom. "He wrote this, if I'm right about the date, during his second trip to rehab." He sighed.

Camila rubbed a hand over his back. "I wonder if some of this could help someone. You know, help educate kids in some anti-drug campaign."

"That's a good idea," James said, letting it take root in his mind. The thought was like a hefty weight placed on one side of a scale. One end represented the doom and gloom side of things. The other being its counter, where hope and encouragement lay. Camila's idea, surprisingly simple as it was, planted a very real layer of hope in him, and James couldn't help but cling to it. Like Winston clung to the rope of freedom in his sketch.

The trick was to let go of the other so it didn't drag him back down.

The next few put a smile on his face. Winston had given each of his siblings a character drawing. Betzy's had a literal heart of gold filled in with some sort of metallic marker or pen. It was the biggest thing on her body, aside from the ultra tall high heels she wore.

Zander's pointed out his obsession for watches. A tiny body with a big head and a giant forearm boasting his collection of watches, everything from Rolex to Gucci to Guess. He got his arched brow spot on.

Duke was sporting a clown nose while performing a juggling act with—*what else?*—women. James couldn't help but laugh.

"He was one witty son of a gun," he mumbled while setting that one aside. And there was his. In his portrait, James had a big head and a massive chest boasting the initials JB. A bright cape flapped in the breeze.

Camila whistled a catcall. "Cute. What's that by your feet?"

James moved his gaze down the page to see for himself. A furry little puffball with beady eyes sat nestled against his superhero boots. He laughed out loud. "That's Frank, my gerbil. I loved that little guy." A deep longing gripped hold of him then. A fresh and sudden urge to talk to Winston about the good old days. And to tell him how much he liked his drawings. He was sorry that he got in so much trouble for doodling at school. Maybe they should have encouraged him instead. Gotten him into more art classes.

Dad wouldn't have been happy to see one of his kids pursue

art over financial education, but if he'd have known where Winston's misfit path would lead him…

He sniffed as moisture welled up in his eyes. Memories of the time they left the school property during recess and made straight for the gas station to pile up on sour gummies and candy corns. Or the time they went horseback riding and Duke got bucked off. Mom almost had a heart attack as she raced in to get him. And James and Winston, they laughed their butts off while Mom dusted him off.

"Dang, I miss him so bad." The sad truth was, he'd been missing his brother before the overdose. In many ways, Winston had checked out. Become, as his poem suggested, more of a shell.

Camila nodded and sniffed. "I bet. He seems like such a neat guy."

"Yeah, he was." He looked at the pile he'd set aside to share with the rest of his family as a thought came to mind. "I'm almost temped to do the life celebration thing after all," he admitted. "Just going through all of this. Thinking about all the qualities I miss. I don't know, I feel almost…ready, I guess."

"That's great," Camila said, shifting in the seat to face him. "Really, James. That's progress."

He liked the encouragement he saw on her face. It was starting to feel like he and Camila were more of a team. His mind had been making the shift for a while now. Thinking in terms of *us*—him and Camila—instead of *me*. Only this time, the thought didn't spark any triggers or fear. He liked it. Liked knowing he wasn't alone.

"Wow, James," Camila said. "Look at this one." The reverence in her tone told him it might be what he was looking for.

The unknown entry that would bring him some level of comfort of assurance that he hadn't driven his brother over the edge.

He turned his gaze to the drawing she held on a full-sized page. He'd seen only a few others that had been sketched onto the softer, thicker art paper like this. It was a full-body character portrait of Winston. He was standing tall and free and boasting a massive muscle with a wide grin. Broken shackles hung off his ankles. Shackles that, when he followed the attached chains, led to a graveyard of bottles, pills, and syringes laying in his wake. His piercing was reflected in this one, the gold hoop at the outer edge of his brow.

It seemed to echo parts of his tug of war sketch. With the drugs to the far left of the photo. He looked to be walking away from that, and headed toward the opposite side of the picture, where a hand was held out for him.

He stared at it, willing it to give him what he longed to know.

But he found nothing more. No words in the shadows. No dates written along the side.

His gaze moved back to the hand he was walking toward. Who was it supposed to belong to? James' architect friend he planned to shadow? Some guy at the recovery clinic who'd helped him get clean?

But then something came to his attention. The page, as large as it was, had been folded along the edge, hiding about an inch of the picture along the right side. James flattened the edge as a dose of urgency sparked within him.

The page no longer ended with just a hand but evidence of a long sleeved dress shirt. And at the wrist, a very important detail came into view—a diamond crusted cufflink with the initials, JB.

Leaving it all behind. Hello, Cincinnati. JB, thanks for not giving up on me.

Warmth circled his heart at the words. He read them once more, trying to piece it all together. James already knew Winston had been on board at some point, heck, it's why he'd said yes in the first place. But the date...

"Wait, that's the date he died. I mean, by the time the medical examiners got there, they estimated his time of death somewhere around four in the morning."

"What time was it that he texted you?" Camila asked.

"It was well before midnight. I was watching the Laker's game."

"You said you wouldn't tell your architect friend that he was canceling. That Winston would have to tell the guy himself. That means you still had hope he would show. You *hadn't* given up on him, and you didn't want to take part in closing that door."

"Maybe," James said. He knew what she was getting at. It was the same thing James was hoping for. If this had been drawn after their conversation, he'd feel a whole lot better. But how would they ever know?

"Do you know if he ever called to cancel?"

"He must not have, because Tyler called me later that morning, concerned that he hadn't shown."

Camila nodded. "Have you spoken with him since?"

"Not in specifics. I just...the guy came to his funeral, gave his condolences. We've had a few business interactions since then, but that's about it. You think I should contact him? See if

Winston ever reached out?"

"It wouldn't hurt," Camila said.

James nodded as something on the page caught his attention. Faint text seeming to seep from the other side of the page. His heart went numb as he flipped the paper over, revealing another stretch of words penned on the other side—again— right in the once-folded portion. As if he'd *meant* to hide it from view.

Our final dance.
 Our sweet goodbye.
 No more will you control my life.
 One last dance,
 then we'll be through.
 This is the last I'll see of YOU.

A dark chill shook James to the core. He hadn't missed the similarities to the other poem. The way he'd compared his addiction to a dance. Winston *had* planned to go to Cincinnati after all. But he wanted to have one last hoorah first.

James clenched his fist so tight it hurt. He remembered reading articles on addiction and recovery. He'd once read of a guy who'd gotten clean, like Winston. Something happened down the road, he lost a girlfriend perhaps. And the guy relapsed. Officials believe he used the same amount he'd been accustomed to, but the tolerance for it was no longer there. He overdosed, leaving his family to grieve the loss of a fighter who, inevitably, lost the fight.

That last hurrah had cost Winston his life. Somewhere in his mind, James realized it would take years to process the truth of it. To accept that Winston had gone into the act so foolishly.

Wordlessly, Camila wrapped her arms around him and leaned into his chest. She might be new to his life, but already, she was familiar. Her candy-like scent, her generous warmth, and the way her silky hair brushed against his cheek when they embraced.

James ran his chin along the length of her upper arm, back and forth, reflecting on the detail he'd just learned. And on the way that, having this woman here by his side, grounded him somehow. Kept him from flying away in that panicky place of desperation and doubt. It forced him to simply sit with what had happened to Winston. The tragedy of it all.

In the quiet moment, he thought back on the seed Camila planted in him earlier. She'd suggested he use Winston's story to help others somehow. He vowed then to do that very thing. Somehow, in the not-too-distant future, James would find ways he could do something about it. If he could possibly deter kids from starting down that crooked path, it'd be a worthwhile cause.

He nodded, brought his lips to Camila's cheek, and planted a kiss where that adorable dimple sank into her cheek. "Thank you," he whispered against her skin. "Thanks for helping me through this."

Camila tipped her head slightly, bringing her mouth to his, and gave him a soft kiss. "Thanks for letting me."

James urged her to lean into him once more as he settled deeper into the beanbag. He would soak up her warmth for a while longer before they said goodnight.

Yet just as his tired eyes started to drift, a flash of lightning lit up the darkened sky. A thunderous boom followed, crashing angrily over the beach. It felt as if they'd entered the heart of a drum as the roar intensified. The glass took on a response of its own—the windows and skylights ringing the raging echo with every shiver and pulse.

As much as he wanted to prevent it, as much as James tried to keep it out, that sliver of fear snuck back into his heart. Cold. Dark. Sharp.

The storm was ready to do its worst.

A recollection of Stephanie's warning texts came to mind. Hopefully the downpour outside would be the only storm he had to weather; James had been through enough heartache to last him a very long time. And if what Camila told him was true, so had she.

CHAPTER 20

*J*ames' favorite tunes flowed through his earbuds as he ran along the sandy beach. He liked how his Bowie mix reminded him of Camila, liked how they'd made a lot of memories to the very same songs.

Yesterday, he'd told Camila that he loved her, and boy had he meant it. Some might argue that that three weeks wasn't enough time to fall in love with someone. He might have argued that himself. But James knew better now. Knew that nights and days with Camila by his side were the best he'd known. And he couldn't wait to get back to life in LA and make her part of that world too.

He'd texted his family just that morning. Told them of his plans for a life celebration party at Grandpa's cabin by the lake. He'd introduce the family to Camila, and have her by his side as he celebrated the lives of both Dad and Winston. It was no longer a thing of dread, rather something to look forward to.

Having his family come to love Camila as he did—that would be the icing on the cake. Hopefully for her as well; after all, she didn't really have a family of her own. Not anymore.

The thought made him all the more glad she'd be part of his family now. Sure, he might be jumping the gun in thinking on a future together. Heck, not one of his siblings had married yet, and he was the youngest one living. But what good was being in love with a woman if you couldn't see a future with her?

A loud, pulsing buzz interrupted the final song on his workout playlist as he neared the villa. James pulled the phone from his pocket and tugged an ear bud from his ear. *Caller Unknown.*

He sent the thing to voicemail. This wasn't his personal phone, which meant the unknown caller likely had the wrong number. But just as he went to tuck the phone back into his pocket, a text came in.

Unknown Caller: *James, answer the phone, please.*

James: *Who is this?*

Unknown Caller: *Adel. Call me.*

James couldn't hold back the eye roll. Adel was the last person he wanted to talk to right then. But the fact was, they *did* need to talk. Mainly, he wanted to get Adel on the same page. She was dating several men across the globe, since they never had been committed to one another, but James wanted to keep his name clear of hers in the tabloids from that point on. Make it clear that the two of them weren't together.

He gave the screen a few taps, prompted it to get Adel on the line, and put it on speaker as another text came in.

"James?" Adel answered. "Did you see my latest text?"

James squinted against the sun at the screen. She'd sent him an image. He tapped on it so it would fill the screen. Looked like a copy of some signed document or other.

"I got it," he said, scanning quickly through the words on the document. "This is a submission to get on the Lion's Den."

"Right," she said. "There are two parts. I'm sending the other one now."

James couldn't imagine why Adel would be forwarding such a thing onto him, unless she'd run into someone who'd auditioned for the show and been rejected. Perhaps she wanted to pull a favor on a friend's behalf.

He hurried onto the second page of the application, but stiffened as he registered what he'd just seen. With one quick swipe, the first page came back into view. The portion that had been filled in with blue ink. It was the name that had caught his eye. *Camila Lopez.*

A hot and hollow ache tore through his chest as he stared at her name, trying to figure out what it meant.

"I guess you guys did some…stretch on the show where you paid off college loans or something?"

He nodded. "Yes. A couple years ago. It was for self-employed graduates. We were investing in their small businesses too."

"Well, the chick you're dating applied for it, but she got turned down."

There were too many details in that sentence to unpack them all. "How did you know we were dating?"

"You've been spotted on Myrtle Beach by a ton of tourists, James. Are you *seriously* dating that clumsy chef from

Shimwah's party? I mean, you *do* know that *you're* the reason you and I are not a thing, right? You could have *me* anytime you want. Don't act like I haven't made that clear."

She'd made it clear, all right. James just hadn't been interested. But still, someplace in the back of his mind, an image of what was happening began to unfold.

Adel couldn't have gotten this information on her own. Which meant someone had put her up to it. And James knew exactly who that somebody was.

"Did Stephanie send this to you?" he asked.

The line went quiet.

"Adel?"

"Maybe. What difference does it make? You're dating a poor little gold digger who couldn't get money by getting onto your show. *This* is her Plan B."

A new explosion of heat ripped through his chest at the thought. "That's not true." And perhaps it wasn't. Stephanie had been trying to get dirt on Camila since day one. Was it possible Stephanie had set all of this up? Filled out a form to make it look like Camila had applied for the show?

James pulled the documents up on his phone once more. He'd seen Camila's signature before, enough to know that she always used a heart to dot the 'I'.

With frantic fingers, he scanned to the second page, scrolled down the bottom, and zoomed in on the signature beside the X.

And there it was. Camila's round, cursive script, tall and precise. And there, nestled between the letters, was that tiny heart.

His pulse raced hard and fast.

How could seeing something with his eyes make his whole body hurt? The ache was everywhere but nowhere all at once.

She really had tried out for the show.

"There's a reason you don't date women like her," Adel chirped. "They're too much of a risk."

His eyes were starting to blur. Gone was the crisp view of the ocean meeting the shore. He could hardly make out the villa just yards away.

Throat tightening, his pulse climbing faster with each breath, James lowered himself onto the sand. "I really don't think she's like that." He was saying it more to himself, but Adel replied with a trill of laughter.

"I'm sure you don't. Listen, this doesn't look good. For either of us, really. The sooner you can send her packing, the better. Goodbye, James."

The phone went dead, leaving him with his thoughts in a wild whirl. What did this mean? That Camila hadn't been upfront with him?

But that didn't mean she'd done something scandalous, right? In fact, who could blame her for auditioning for the episode? Anyone with school loans and a small business would be a fool *not* to try out for it. Camila was a confident, assertive woman who—had it been up to him—would have made it all the way to that stage.

He nodded, forcing his next breath to come out paced and slow.

It was the fact that she hadn't told him. That's what bothered him most. Not that he could blame her. It might be embarrassing to admit it. Especially since she knew James and his family were leery of people wanting them for their money.

So now what?

He looked down at the application once more, focused on the digits beside her debt, and wondered how much of that she owed even still.

What it came down to was truth. So, would Camila—if given the chance—come clean about applying to get on the show? James felt confident that she would. If she did, James wouldn't hold it against her. He'd be willing to forgive the fact that she'd hidden it up to that point.

But what if she didn't come clean?

He clenched his eyes shut and groaned. If Camila refused to fess up, he'd be left with just one possible assumption: that she couldn't be trusted.

James stayed put for a while longer, hesitant to disrupt his elevated image of Camila. Of the person he'd built her up to be. Soon, he'd get up, dust the sand off his hands, and head back to the villa. Soon, he'd ask for the answer he dreaded to hear.

But for now, James would see Camila as the innocent, passionate, and honest woman he'd fallen in love with. For just a moment more, he'd hold onto hope.

Camila towel-dried her hair while eyeing the bright blue sky through the window. Last night's storm had nearly gotten the best of her. Its noisy rain, relentless wind, and shocking claps of thunder had her wanting to venture out of her room and into James' room instead. Sure, she'd wanted to cuddle up to him during the chaos, but more than that, Camila had something to get off her chest.

It didn't feel right to keep parts of her past from him. Not when he'd been so open about the darkness in his own past. Still, yesterday had belonged to James and Winston. He'd finally got the resolution he'd been looking for.

In a way, yesterday would belong to her and James too. To their relationship. It marked the day they'd confessed their love for one another, and that was a day she wouldn't soon forget.

The mere recollection made her sigh with warmth, happiness, and hope. And as she let her mind drift to the moments that followed, when James backed her against the doors and kissed her long and slow, a new sort of heat pushed through her.

James was spectacular. He knew how to make her feel wanted in all the right ways. Wanted as a woman, as a partner, as a friend. As an important part in his life. She'd had random pieces of that puzzle, scattered between one relationship to the next, but never had Camila enjoyed all of those qualities in one, rewarding relationship. She could finally see what kept her grandparents going all those years. And she hoped, very much, that James might be the person she'd spend similar years with as well.

Hopefully, what she shared with him today wouldn't scare him away. She doubted it would. James was loving and compassionate. She knew that much by now. He'd be more concerned about her and what she'd dealt with than how it might taint his own image. At least, she hoped.

Today, she'd make time to let him know the details behind her parents' death. Already, she looked forward to having the task off her chest once and for all.

She turned her mind to the breakfast menu. Camila had set

aside some roasted potatoes from last night's dinner, and she planned to mash them up with crumbled bacon, grated cheese, sour cream and chives. After shaping the mixture into patties, she'd batter and fry them until golden brown. Fried slices of yellow squash tossed with fresh, diced tomatoes would make for the perfect side dish.

In less than a week, they'd be back in LA, settling into a life of juggling work and their blooming relationship. And while Camila had reservations about what that transition might look like, she felt confident that they'd make one another priority. After all, they'd spent nearly every waking hour together for close to a month now. Aside from their romantic connection, they were friends. James had already invited her to come to his family's annual life celebration gathering. She could hardly wait to meet the family members she'd heard so much about.

Camila was also looking forward to having a candid conversation with Gypsy about the billionaire she'd met at The Royal Palm. About who he was to her now. Thank heavens her young friend had been tied up in an adventure of her own, flying off to the Bahamas for her yoga study. She was staying in tents on the beach, cooking meals for a group over an open flame, and living a life that suited her free-spirited friend very well.

"Camila, can I talk to you for a moment, please?"

She glanced up to see James standing in the kitchen entryway. His posture was off, restless. Tight in the shoulders, weight shifting from foot to foot. That, combined with the somber tone of his voice, sparked a knot of fear in Camila's gut.

She set the freshly washed tomato onto the counter and used the apron to dry off her hands. "What's wrong, James?"

That's when she noticed that deep furrow in his brow. It was a look she hadn't seen him in since…since his appearance on the live television show.

"Hopefully nothing." He motioned to the dining area. "Let's…step over to the table, if you don't mind."

It was such a formal suggestion that it made her bristle. It reminded her of the way he'd tried to reason with her when she'd first arrived. Some attempt to keep things civilized.

Camila's heart skipped a beat. "Why would we need to sit down?" She'd tried to put a touch of humor in the query, but it came out more accusing instead. That knot of anxiety swelled larger. Hotter. Began gnawing at her from the inside. "C'mon, James. Let's just talk right here."

James sighed, his shoulders dropping as he took two long strides into the kitchen. He locked his eyes on her. "Are you hiding something from me?"

Her breath hitched. A bomb had just gone off in her chest, she was sure of it. Camila managed a nod as she tried to form the words. He'd found out about her parents. Found out before she could even tell him. She should never have waited so long.

"Yes," she finally admitted. "There is something I haven't told you." She was halfway through the sentence when James sighed with relief. It made her pause for a blink, but then she continued. "I've been trying to think of a way to bring this up all week, but I haven't found the right time."

"Good," James said. "And I'm only bringing this up because, well, you know that I have to be careful about who I trust."

Camila nodded, hoping he wouldn't be so worried about his image that he couldn't see past it. Hoping that he wouldn't respond the way some of her middle school classmates did when they found out about it.

James rested an arm on the counter, seeming more at ease now. "You saw Winston's drawing about Melanie, right? She was totally using him for his money. You've never given me cause to think you're that way, but hearing that you applied to get onto The Lion's Den last year kind of freaked me out."

Wait, what?

"Mainly because you didn't tell me. In fact…" He pulled back from the counter and straightened as something sparked in his eyes. "You told me you didn't even know who I was…"

"James, I never applied to get on The Lion's Den. I mean, I'd heard about the show, but I hadn't even seen an episode until after we bumped into each other."

She studied his reaction as the words left her lips. The subtle shake of his head. Tightening of his jaw. The clench of one fist. "Try again, Camila. Just…tell me the truth and we can move on from this. *Please.*"

Her throat went dry, as if it might clamp up around the words seeking an escape. "I *am* telling the truth." She hurried around the counter and reached for his arm, but James took a sharp step back.

"You just admitted you were hiding something."

"Not *that,*" she assured. But she was too derailed to even think. There was no point going into what she wanted to tell him if he believed she was lying to him about something else.

"So you're hiding *two* things from me then," he accused. "Sounds like I don't know you as well as I thought I did."

"That's not true," she said, her voice shaky and weak.

"I know for a fact that you tried to get on the show." He was gaining momentum now. She could sense it in the growing volume of his voice. "I give you a chance to come clean about it, hoping we can just get past it and move on, but you lie about it instead."

She shook her head, unable to even find the words to defend herself. It was all so shocking. So…out of the blue.

"You're wrong," she assured, but James piped up once more.

"And then I find out that there's a whole other secret you want to come clean with? Probably to distract me from the fact that you're not the woman you painted yourself to be."

Camila's lips were parted, her mouth poised to defend herself and tell James just how wrong he was. But that last line silenced her. The woman she'd *painted* herself to be? Did the truth about her parents play a defining factor in that equation?

She shook her head, pressed her lips together, and scrambled for an effective way to defend herself. "Maybe we *should* sit down," she blurted. "We need to figure out where you got the impression that I—"

"It's not just an impression, Camila. It's a fact. I have proof. You know, I can work with problems. I do that with companies all day long. Take a look at what's broken and see if we can fix it. But if I don't have all the facts…if I'm dealing with a bunch of lies about who you are and what you've done—there's nothing I can do."

"James, just tell me where you heard that."

He held her gaze for a blink, his blue eyes rimmed with red. Moisture welled at the corners, but it wasn't enough to blur their dark and hollow state. "I think you should leave."

Camila covered a gasp as her heart sank. For all the fight

Camila had within her, for all the passion for justice and rightness and good, she couldn't muster enough to speak.

"I'll pay for your flight back home, and for the remainder of the week as well. Just…make your exit as brief as possible." He spun away from her then, but paused before walking out. He tipped his head, allowing a glimpse of his profile. "Goodbye, Camila."

CHAPTER 21

*I*t felt like Camila was walking in someone else's shoes. Not in the sense that she was in a new place experiencing a different life. The surroundings of her LA apartment said it all. She was in her own home with all the familiar comforts surrounding her.

But there was no comfort to be found. And as she pulled her clothes from the suitcase and piled them into the washer, it felt as if she was moving someone else's arms. And when she walked over to the sink, filled up a glass to water the plant, it felt like she was using someone else's feet.

Her body had gone into retreat mode. Numbed itself to any real sensation. Hoping to stop the impending pain from settling in.

James had sent her packing. But not before he'd accused her of lying about trying to get onto his family's show. Something she'd never even considered doing.

She was glad Gypsy wasn't home yet. The two would've gotten back around the same time had Camila finished out her month at the Royal Palm, but now she'd have some time alone to sit with what had happened. To accept that James—the man she'd fallen in love with—had broken things off.

She wasn't sure when it would really hit her. Camila had figured it might sink in once she was in the town car. Or on the plane. But that stubborn strand of disbelief held out.

A sharp whistle broke into her thoughts, reminding Camila that she'd placed the kettle on the stove. She hurried over to shut off the heat and snatch a mug from the cupboard. After dropping a bag of licorice tea into the mug, she filled it up and set a plate on top to let it steep.

She snatched the pile of mail off the table, tossed it onto the tray with her tea, and wandered onto her back patio. A soft breeze blew over the evening sky. For a moment, she expected a different view—the view she'd become accustomed to seeing from the patio at the Villa.

At once, she recalled the first time James invited her to join him for breakfast. The sincere apology he'd offered over what Adel had done. A whirlwind of memories followed. Everything from their first, playful kiss on the beach, to the moment James had confessed his love for her.

It had been such a beautiful love story.

The vision of a future with him had been so clear, as crazy as that was with their differences. But the things that mattered —what they wanted out of life—those things were the same. Of course, she didn't share his obsession for watermelon...

A bout of laughter spilled from her lips. "He's obsessed with that freaking watermelon." She shook her head, picturing the many times she'd seen him sneaking into the kitchen for the stash she'd placed in the fridge. The way he turned into a foodie while grading the quality of each new melon.

And suddenly the smiles and laughter were gone. Replaced by a flow of tears and sobs as the pain struck at last—a sudden ache ripping through her chest.

James was gone.

He wasn't part of her today, and he wouldn't be part of her tomorrow. Even worse, the joy she'd felt in all the yesterdays— that was tarnished. It was like discovering the end to a book while reading along the way. Only to find that it wouldn't give her the happily ever after she'd hoped for.

Her thoughts rushed back to her last moments at the villa. The rush to get out of there in her frazzled state. The busy hustle of getting to the airport. The day was all but gone, and it was only now hitting her.

In a way, it was a relief. The inevitable grieving process had begun. Who knew how long it would last, or if she'd ever fully recover from a loss so deep, especially when that loss was based on a total misunderstanding.

Her mind flashed to a moment when she and Gypsy had been sitting in this very spot just before she left. It was when Gypsy discovered the video clip of James losing his cool on the show. A recollection sparked in her mind, but slipped away before Camila could grip hold of it.

It was probably nothing. Yet as she lifted the mug to her lips, inhaling the scent of her tea, it came back to her. Gypsy's off comment: *Good thing you never got onto that show. He probably would have bit your head off.*

"Wait…" Camila said as it came together in her mind. Gypsy

had been known to do some pretty sneaky things. Especially if she felt it would better the life of a friend. So that led to one very important question. One she wouldn't have an answer to until Gypsy got home: Had her friend filled out a form for The Lion's Den on Camila's behalf?

CHAPTER 22

$\mathcal{J}$ames scrolled down the screen on his laptop, eyes aching and dry as he checked the numbers of one of his recent rescue attempts from The Lion's Den —a large industrial plant that was finally starting to work its way back into the black. Not much had changed since he scrutinized the numbers yesterday, but it was good to keep a close eye on them. Perhaps he should take a second look at the others too. A quick glance at the clock said it'd been over twelve hours since he'd done so.

That glance also said that he should have left the office hours ago, but James couldn't pull himself away from the leather chair, oak desk, and the rest of the setting that gave his brain the very crucial message that it was time to focus on things of business—not personal. Not Camila Lopez, the woman who—despite his greatest efforts—still owned the lion's share of his heart.

Back at home, James could let his mind wander to the

dimple that sank into her cheek when she grinned at him. The way she'd talk about food in that low, sultry voice. The way she ran her fingers through his hair when they kissed...

He cleared his throat and straightened in his seat, hoping to banish the images from his brain. This was his safe place, after all. *Yeah, right.*

Since he'd left the villa a week ago, shortly after Camila took her exit, James had discovered there *were* no safe places. There was no escape from the hellish torment of what he'd both gained and lost in the space of three and a half weeks.

At one point, Duke had said that what happened at the Royal Palm was supposed to stay at the Royal Palm. So much for that idea. The office had been bombarded with phone calls and emails alike with inquiries about his relationship with the pretty private chef from the Royal Palm. That in itself wasn't the problem. What James hated most about the questions involving his relationship is that there was no longer a relationship to speak of.

James' cell phone gave out a quiet buzz from where it sat, face up, on the desk. A text.

Stephanie: *Almost done burning the midnight oil? How about we grab a drink?*

A knot of dread came over him as he reread the text. As if the act would suddenly change his answer. Stephanie was a hard worker, one who rarely left the office before he did. The two had grabbed drinks after work more times than he could count. He was usually anxious to rehash the latest digits after a long day at work, and who better to do that with than someone who knew every company he was dealing with, win or fail.

Just do it, James. Maybe it will help you get out of your head. He nodded, surprised he was even considering it. In one sense, he was still angry with her. But the better part of him knew he was bitter more than anything else. And Stephanie wasn't the cause of that.

Besides, what could it hurt? It was better than going home to his empty house and obsessing over his breakup for the rest of the night.

James: *Sure. Give me another ten minutes to wrap things up.*

Stephanie sent back a thumbs-up emoji. James stared at it while a recollection came to mind. One he'd tried very hard to bury over the last week. It was just that—Camila had said there was something she'd been meaning to tell him. Something other than what he'd hoped she'd reveal. But he hadn't yet discovered what that was. On more than one occasion, James had assumed it was probably the very detail Stephanie had been trying to share. All it would take was a simple question, and James would have his answer. He was well aware of that fact. But he hadn't been willing to ask. Hadn't been ready to hear.

But now, after a week had gone by since he'd looked into those brown eyes, heard her tempt him with her latest culinary creation, James was aching for more of Camila. Even if it was details he might wish he hadn't known.

During his flight back to LA, James had gone over every detail of Camila's application—the one she'd denied ever sending. It turned out that—while she owed money for her school loans—she didn't meet the minimum requirement for the show. So she'd requested the producers give the difference to her favorite charity instead. A program designed to help foster kids in the community.

James wasted no time in researching the charity himself.

Camila had arranged to conduct monthly cooking classes with the local kids in foster care, involving other chefs in the area too. Not only that, Camila had—according to a news article he'd found—lined up a list of other opportunities as well. Music lessons by talented musicians willing to donate their time, local photographers, artists, and more.

At one point, she'd even appeared on a morning news program where she cooked with the kids in front of the camera. Halloween treats for an upcoming fundraiser the station was promoting last year.

The mere recollection brought that gut-punching ache back in a blink. How could someone so beautiful possess such a deceptive bone in her body? Since leaving the villa, James had been tempted to give up his bias, see past the offense, and chalk it up to some sort of brain cramp on Camila's part—as if she'd simply forgotten that she had, in fact, turned in an application after all. But that would make him a fool.

Still, he'd resorted to stalking her on social media. Reading articles from her food blog. Scrolling past pictures of pretty food with descriptions that gave him much-needed doses of that addictive passion he loved so much.

It was easy to hear her voice in his mind as he read. And while he knew he'd pay the price for it later—he always did— James gave in to those moments just the same. The connection made him feel closer to her. Closer to himself again too. During his time with Camila, James had caught a glimpse of the man he was meant to become. But already the image was starting to fade, morph back into the workaholic he'd turned into since Winston's death.

A deep ache settled over his left temple. James came to a

stand. Better his head than his heart. The idea caused a dark chuckle to sound in his throat. His heart *was* hurting. In ways he'd never known. Which didn't make a whole lot of sense to him. Loss was loss, right? And he'd lost before. His own blood.

He wanted to numb it. To turn the drink he'd grab on the way home into half a dozen drinks instead. James had never been one to rely on alcohol to dull the pain, especially in light of Winston's substance abuse, but the temptation was gaining merit. What was the harm in shutting his pain out for just one night?

That very question ran through his head as he and Stephanie climbed into the back of the car.

"Thanks, Leonard," he said with a nod before his driver closed the door.

The nightlife beyond the tinted windows welcomed James with a promise. Neon street signs, busy sidewalks, and head-lights from passing cars. There was a life outside of the night-mare he was stuck in. He just needed to reach out and take it.

"Did you see the numbers from the Bronson deal?" Stephanie asked.

The question made him realize they hadn't spoken since getting in the car.

"Yeah," he said. "Looking good."

"Good? Incredible is more like it. Unbeatable. I've got to hand it to you—you really turned that one around. I'm impressed."

He nodded. "Thank you." He glanced out the window as they pulled up to a light. A set of double doors, bright against the night, caught his attention. He wasn't sure why; the street was crowded with shoppers and passersby alike. But as his gaze settled on just one spot behind those doors, a woman came into view. A very beautiful woman who looked a whole lot like Camila. Caramel colored skin, long brown hair, and that curvy figure.

A bolt of lightning shot through his chest as he pulled away from the seat and brought his face close to the window. It *was* her. That was Camila. A near-absent glance above the doors as they proceeded into the intersection said she was at a kitchen supplies shop. Another indicator that it was, in fact, her.

It felt as if that horrendous thunderstorm—the storm that raged on the day he'd said he loved her—was back in full force. Stuck in the confines of his chest. He gulped hard, rubbed his palms over his slacks, and fought the intense and growing urge to have Leonard pull over and let him out.

Camila was right there. She was actually just yards from him. And he was sitting in some stupid limo driving on by like a moron? It brought back the question he wanted to ask Stephanie.

"When I was at the villa, before Adel sent me the application," James started, "you sent me something to me about Camila's past. What was it?"

A green glow illuminated Stephanie's face as they passed a bright neon sign. "You never read it?"

James shook his head.

Stephanie dropped her gaze to her lap, ran a finger along the tips of her long, red fingernails. "Does it matter anymore?" she asked without looking up.

Even as shadows moved over her face, James saw the hurt in her eyes. Heard it in her voice. "Yes," he answered. "It matters to me."

Stephanie leaned forward, snatched her phone from her bright red bag, and tapped at the screen. "It's better for you to read it for yourself. I'll resend it."

A second later his phone buzzed with the text.

Stephanie shifted in her seat until her body faced the door. Her earrings dangled in her silhouette, the tear-shaped planes catching reflections of headlights as they passed.

Sensing she was giving him a moment to himself, James tapped the screen to bring up the attachment she'd sent him. He watched as it pulled up an old newspaper printout. *Man Murders Wife Then Turns Gun on Self.*

His brow furrowed as he looked over it. Stephanie must have sent him the wrong one by accident. Or perhaps the relevant article was beneath this one.

But then a detail jumped out at him. *The pair's young daughter, just three years old, had been staying with her grandparents during the incident. An official on the scene said that might have been the child's saving grace.*

James checked the date on the article as it started to sink in; the math was spot on.

His stomach sank. A shallow thud echoed in his ears. One massive clank after the next as chills crawled up his arms.

He tore through the remainder of the piece as the words grew blurry, the devastation within him growing even still.

His eyes clenched shut. "Camila," he said in a whisper. His mind uttered what he couldn't say aloud. *I'm so sorry that happened to you. I'm sorry you couldn't tell me. I'm sorry that you wanted to hide it. I want to stop this car, run down the LA sidewalk, throw my arms around you and never let go.*

"James?"

The sound of his name pulled him from his musings. He smeared a hand over his face.

"We're here," Stephanie said. "Are you ready?"

And so they were. In fact, Leonard already held the door open for Stephanie to step out.

Every part of him wanted to say no. He *wasn't* ready to walk into that club, sink into some lounge chair, and kick back drinks. He *wasn't* ready to shove his mind back on work like he had when Winston died. To pretend it *didn't* feel like his heart was getting ripped into oblivion. He wasn't ready to let go of the woman he'd fallen so in love with that he barely knew how to breathe without her.

"Mr. Benton?" Leonard urged.

James gulped hard, tucked his phone back into his suit coat pocket, and slid across the leather seat toward Stephanie. "Yeah," he lied. "I'm ready."

CHAPTER 23

*C*amila slid the final crate into the back of her hatchback car before stepping back to look over her list.

"It's all there, I promise," Gypsy said. "Now can we please just talk about this whole thing so I can move on with my life? I'm never going to be able to forgive myself."

Camila had made it to the center of her checklist, but her friends' words yanked her attention from the page. She looked up at her, summoned the most pathetic-looking plea she could, and repeated what she'd told her already a hundred times.

"Gypsy, you have *nothing* to apologize for. Did you submit that application to make my life better?"

"Yeah, but—"

Camila lifted a finger to stop her. "Yes or no."

Sunlight bounced off Gypsy's blonde bob as she nodded. Her streaks, now pink instead of blue, did the same. "Yes."

"And were you also trying to better the lives of the foster kids in my program?"

"You're making it sound like I'm a saint and we both know I'm far from it."

Camila reached out, tossed her arms around her sweet friend, and gave in to a laugh. It was better than giving in to the tears she'd let loose more times than she could count. "I wish I hadn't told you the part about the Lion's Den. If I could've solved this thing without telling you, I would have. But I just needed to know."

Gypsy rubbed Camila's back before giving it a few pats. "Well, I still think he's stupid for losing you over it. Mark my words, James Benton will see you as the one who got away until the day he dies." She squished her tighter before pulling away. "Unless he comes to his senses and gets you back somehow."

Camila hated the desperate part of her that rejoiced in the idea. "That won't happen, but that's okay. I'm not sure I even *want* that to happen." *Lie.* "This whole experience has given me a glimpse into the mistrusting mind of a billionaire. The truth is, he has good reason to mistrust people. Over a billion good reasons, actually."

Gypsy nodded and peeked into the back of the car. "Well, at least he helped you get back in business. You're cooking for Shane freaking Faretti. That's, like, amazing."

Yes, it was. And Camila was grateful for it. "You're right. Speaking of which," she said with a quick glance at the time.

"Yeah, yeah. You've got to go. I know. I still wish you'd let me make it right with the billionaire," Gypsy hollered as Camila climbed behind the wheel.

Camila turned the engine over, but she was quick to roll

down the window as she did. "That's off limits, Gypsy. Please tell me you understand how much I would never ever *ever* be able to forgive you if I found out you tried to tell him about it."

Camila kept her foot on the brake, a sick knot of panic twisting in her gut as she waited for Gypsy's response.

"I understand," she said with a nod.

Camila gave her a nod in return, but it would take a whole lot of deep breaths to soften the tension in her arms, shoulders, and chest. There was a very good reason she didn't want to make excuses for her application on the Lion's Den. Camila feared it would come across all wrong. James might not see it as an explanation for why the application had come through. Rather a devious attempt to deny what she'd essentially been accused of—wanting his money over him.

There was a second reason too. One that went all the way back to the small child who doubted her mother's love for her. What if James didn't really love her the way she'd thought he had? What if he was simply using the incident as an excuse to be done with her now that their time at the resort was through? She couldn't fathom the idea of clearing up the misunderstanding only to have James shrug it off and move onto a life without her in it.

With her phone propped into place and navigating the course, Camila made her way to the home of world-famous tennis player, Shane Faretti. She was mentally running over the things she'd need to do once she arrived when Cyree called.

Just one look at the screen sent Camila's mind to shoot off in a million different directions. Or maybe that wasn't true. It went directly to *one* very prominent direction: James.

She accepted the call with a quick tap, allowing the line to come in on her speaker. "Hello?"

"Have you taken a look at your bank account?"

Camila shot another look at the name on the screen. Still Cyree. "What? Why?"

"Because Mr. Benton left you one heck of a tip, that's why."

Butterflies swirled wildly around Camila's heart. "He did?" *Stop it, Camila. Don't get excited over it.*

"Most leave about twenty percent. Some give more. Some give less. But I've never seen anyone double the entire wage and call it a tip."

"He gave me double?"

"Yep."

Camila's dumb heart was confused about what this meant. Why did this feel like such a flattering thing? It wasn't. In fact, it almost confirmed that he thought she was after his money so he gave her more of it.

"Cyree?" Her phone dinged, alerting Camila that she needed to get onto the freeway. She wanted to be through with the call before getting up speed, so she circled around the block instead, shadows of palm trees stretching across the hood of her car as she turned.

"Yeah?"

"Can I reject the tip?"

"I don't see how," Cyree said, her voice cautious. "It's already in your account."

Little sparks of frustration crackled through her as she considered that. It didn't seem fair for James to have the last word. Especially when that word was basically saying that he was giving her what she'd wanted most—money.

Cyree still waited on the line.

"Can't I just…give it back to him?"

A sigh sounded through the speaker. "I would strongly advise against that. I think it would offend him."

"Well, maybe *I'm* offended by the tip." Camila sounded silly enough to gain herself an eye roll. "I mean, I'm thankful for it, and I'm flattered. But I'd rather not accept a sum so large."

"It's not that large when you consider the source," Cyree assured. "Just take some time to consider before doing anything rash, okay? That's my suggestion. And if you sincerely don't want the money, you might consider using the funds for your charity."

"That's a good idea," Camila said with a nod. "Very good, actually." She was approaching the interstate again. "I really appreciate you, Cyree. That job has helped me out a ton."

"I'm happy to have helped. I hope we can have you back out here soon."

Camila sighed as a sudden longing pushed through her. "I hope so too." But what she really hoped is that one day she'd be able to enjoy the memories she and James had made together. She might not have gotten those full twenty-eight days with him, and her time hadn't ended in the way that she'd hoped, but Camila would give anything to replay them all the same. To go back to day one, and start all over again.

Her breakup with James had caused more heartache than she thought possible, for knowing a man for less than a month, but there was one thing Camila was certain of: if she could go back and reject the job offer, save herself the trouble and pain, she wouldn't. Despite the loss and sorrow she'd endured, Camila would definitely do it all again.

CHAPTER 24

*J*ames hurried out of his car and toward the back
entrance of the studio with two important people
on his mind. Winston and Camila. Winston,
because he'd be addressing his tragic overdose on live TV. And
Camila, because she's the one who inspired him to do it. And
the truth was, thoughts of Camila were still commonplace for
James.

And he liked it that way. Call him a martyr or glutton for
punishment or an outright fool, but James made a habit of
reliving his time with her at the Villa. They were, after all, the
best days of his life. Even if they'd resulted in some of the
lowest days he'd lived.

The history of Camila's parents, found by the private inves-
tigator Stephanie had hired, had led James to a new discovery—
a published poem written by her very own mother before she
died. One that had clearly been written for Camila. He couldn't

be sure, but he was almost positive Camila didn't know about it. Somehow or other, he planned to change that.

"Mr. Benton," a voice came from behind. James almost dismissed it as paparazzi until he realized they weren't allowed on the property. He paused, spun on one heel, and caught sight of a woman he recognized right away. He'd never seen Gypsy in person, but he'd seen enough pictures, heard enough stories, to recognize both the platinum hair and the spark of mischief in her eye.

"Yes?" he said, stepping away from the entrance and back toward the lot.

The woman stood next to a green VW bug, clenching her fists and standing on her toes. "I have something to tell you. Camila asked me *not* to, but I feel like I owe you the truth, so…"

James gulped past the hard knot rising in his throat. "Okay," he said. "Go ahead." Only he wasn't sure he could take it. He couldn't fathom hearing something that might damage his memories with her. Whatever it was, he hoped that they would survive.

"She's not the one who sent in that application to the Lion's Den. I am." She raised her hand in the air briefly before lowering it back by her side. "I was at a yoga retreat, so Camila wasn't able to piece it all together until I got back, but even still she refused to call and tell you."

James mind was swimming in the pool of new information. Gypsy had been the one to send it in?

"I didn't say anything to Camila because I knew she'd be mad about it, but I figured that if she made it onto the show and ended up getting her loans paid off and the money for her charity…" She shrugged and tipped her head to one side. "How could she be mad about that, right? But they never called so I figured it was just a thing of the past."

He nodded as it sunk further in. "That's good to know," he said, testing out the words for himself. It was, wasn't it? So why did he feel so...hopeless suddenly? The answer came in the form of another question. "Why didn't she want to tell me this herself? I wish she would've just called me and told me the second she found out."

Gypsy blinked, nodded, and looked down at the combat boots on her feet. The lace from her skirt grazed the tops as a breeze blew. "The worst thing anyone could ever think about Camila, from her point of view, is that she's using them. It's just not who she is. I think she assumes that..." She looked up at him through her lashes. "That if you felt like she was capable of that, you probably weren't the right person for her."

A miserable pain stabbed into his chest at the words.

"Which I don't even think is fair," Gypsy blurted. "What else could you assume but that she was lying to you? If I were you, I wouldn't have been able to talk my way around that kind of proof. You had her signature there and everything."

His brow furrowed. "Yes."

The corner of her lip curved down. "I traced it."

He knew it was time to get prepped for the show, that there was a makeup artist waiting and a stage manager pacing, but James couldn't get himself to walk away from this person who was, essentially, the closest thing to family Camila had. "How is she doing?"

Gypsy shook her head. "Ever seen the Living Dead?"

James cringed.

"It's like, she's doing life every day. And she's glad to have clients again and everything, but that passionate spark in her—well, it's actually more like a flame—that's sort of…gone."

It was hard to think beyond that statement. Hard to think about things like Winston and the live interview he was about to give. "Where is she right now?" he asked. His temple was pounding to the point it hurt. It was a mere echo of the crashing reaction in his chest.

"She's on her way to Shane Faretti's. It's prep work for now; the party doesn't start until later."

He nodded as an idea bounced in his brain. He and Shane had been friends for years. In fact, James was the one who'd given Shane the referral just last week. "Thank you." He reached out to shake Gypsy's hand. "I better get inside now."

"Are you going to tell her that I told you?"

James held her gaze for a blink. "Yes. Is that okay?"

Gypsy bit her lip. "I guess it's the same thing as her getting on the show. If it helps her get you back, how can she be mad at me?"

He chuckled. "Good thinking." He hurried back toward the entrance and, as the door drew closed behind him, James heard one last inquiry slip through the door.

"Will it? Help her get you back?"

He wasn't able to turn back and give Gypsy the answer, but if all went well, Camila's friend would discover the answer to that very soon.

CHAPTER 25

*C*amila stared at the massive melon before her, scolding herself for the new obsession she'd found. It seemed that if she couldn't have James, she'd find ways to infuse him into her life just the same. Like with today's dish. A chilled slice of watermelon with crumbled goat cheese, spicy walnuts, fresh mint, and a squeeze of lemon.

Camila wished she'd have come up with the dish before leaving the villa; James would have loved it. Loved it so much he wouldn't have let her go. Boy, was she earning a whole lot of eye rolls lately. At times, Camila's thoughts were downright pathetic. Thank heavens nobody else could hear them but her. Even at that, Camila recognized the ones that had no place in her, and she kicked them right out of her head. Successfully so, most of the time.

But the truth was, she had a *right* to feel sorry for herself, didn't she? Sure, Camila was rebuilding her clientele, and sure, she had more money in her bank account than she'd had in ages, but those weren't the things that mattered to her most. And the worst part was, James didn't know her well enough to see that.

It was hard enough to handle the fact that so many people had the wrong idea about her. The general LA public thinking, for a while anyway, that she was nothing more than a clumsy amateur. But this—knowing that James was viewing her in such a false light—hurt much worse. Even still, it would be worse to discover that he'd simply fallen out of love with her.

Camila lowered the watermelon into the deep sink in Shane Faretti's kitchen. She sprayed it with a fruit rinse and rubbed her hands over the smooth surface to clean up the rind. She was just about to rinse off the spray when a large TV, suspended on the other side of the counter, glowed to life.

She stared at it for a blink as the thing switched stations. A quick glance over her shoulder said no one was in the room with her. So just how was all this happening?

A buzz sounded from her phone, drawing her attention to where it lay face-up on the counter. It was from Shane.

Shane Faretti: *Don't mind the TV. We're doing a bit of mainte-nance. It will go off shortly.*

Camila wiped off her hands and tapped out a reply. *Okay. No problem.*

The screen continued to blare with an advertisement for hand soap, another for baby food, and at last it settled on Samantha Pingley's famous daytime talk show. Camila patted the watermelon dry and hoisted it onto the marble chopping block, the talk show fading into the distance as she gauged the thickness for each slice.

Inwardly, she was recalling the many times she'd diced the

sweet melons for James at the resort. She couldn't help but wonder if he was missing her too. What things did he come across that made him think back on their time together?

"Here with the one and only James Benton," a voice came from the screen.

Camila's eyes went wide. She had to be imagining it. Yet as she moved her gaze from the knife to the flat screen, Camila saw that it was, in fact, James sitting across from Samantha Pingley.

It felt as if her hands had gone numb, and possibly the rest of her body too.

"Before the break, you told us about an organization you're partnering with to educate youth on the dangers of drug addiction. You mentioned losing your own brother, Winston Benton, to addiction just last year. Can you explain how the idea to take action came about?"

Camila's muscles clenched up in defense as the camera panned back to James. As if she could somehow buffer the blow of seeing his face. Hearing his voice. Feeling the intense clash of love and loss.

"A dear friend of mine helped me realize that I couldn't hide from the pain forever," James said. "Trust me, I tried. She also encouraged me to speak up about Winston's overdose. To see if we can't prevent this new generation from falling victim to the many forms of addiction."

A burst of warmth rushed over Camila at his words. Their relationship hadn't lasted, but at least something good was coming out of it. Perhaps she wasn't meant to be with James at all. It seemed more likely that their relationship was strictly meant to help James discover this new platform.

She nodded as that thought settled into an almost comfortable place. It hurt, yes. But it wasn't all for naught.

James answered more questions about the organization and how people could get involved. He was partnering with another program as well—one dedicated to helping family members and loved ones of addicts.

Camila needed to finish up her prep, she knew that much. But she also knew she'd given herself a whole lot of extra time. More than she needed by far. So she stayed in place, body shifting from rigid to lax, soaking up the moments of seeing him on screen, live. She'd spent the last dozen days wondering what James was doing in a given moment. But right now, she knew. She was seeing him in real time. He was doing something wonderful for a good cause, and he'd recognized her part in inspiring him.

"We're going to take one more short break," Samantha announced as the camera moved back on her, "but then we're going to shift gears. There's been a lot of talk about James Benton's love life in recent tabloids. The only trouble is, none of that talk has come from the source himself. Join us after this brief message to see if we can finally get the answers we're looking for."

Camila rushed back to the watermelon and took hold of the knife. Operating on autopilot, she sawed through the melon, creating one quarter-inch slice after the next.

What in heavens name was happening right now? James was on a live TV show and he was just about to get grilled about his love life. More specifically, his love life with *her*.

Panic prickled through her from the inside out. Dozens of hot, tiny pokes growing greater in number and bigger in size.

She set down the knife and rinsed her hands, willing the warmth of the water to soothe her anxious nerves.

It was possible he'd make a laughing stock of her, the way Adel had. But Camila felt confident that he wouldn't. James might not be able to trust her, but he would never cause her harm. So what on earth would he say?

She felt a panic attack coming on. The racing heart, rapid breaths, and the tips of her fingers going tingly and numb. She clenched her eyes shut, summoned some strength from the heavens above, and forced her breathing to slow. A quick glance at the clock said that she still had plenty of time to spare.

Good, considering that her energy was seized by the simple act of breathing in the moment.

"Welcome back," Samantha cheered as the show came back on at last. "On The Lion's Den, he's described as the lady's favorite, but does James Benton already have a lady? And—surprise—it might not be the lady you thought." The host turned to face James as the camera panned out to show them both.

"Many of us assumed—due to a stream of public appearances—that you and supermodel Adel Bordeaux were an item, but that's not the case, is it?"

James shook his head. "No."

"And recently, you were spotted on Myrtle Beach with whom some say was your private chef on the resort." Samantha reached out to touch his arm. "Are you willing to confirm or deny whether that's the case?"

James nodded. "Yes, I can confirm that she was, in fact, my private chef at the resort."

The audience let out oohs and ahs. A catcall rang out over the reaction.

"And will this relationship continue here in LA?"

A somber look crossed over his face. "You know, I've made a lot of mistakes in my lifetime," James said. "It took me an entire year to face Winston's death, and even then, I was only able to do it because she stood by my side.

"I fell in love with this woman. I really did. And then I made a mistake. One that might have cost me the relationship."

The studio went quiet, but the voices in Camila's head were making up the difference. *What is he saying? Is this real? Am I sure I'm even awake right now?*

"This time, I don't want to sit around for another year before trying to make it better. So let me just say to her, if she's watching..." James fixed those brooding blue eyes right on the lens.

"I was wrong. And as you know, I *like* knowing when I'm wrong because it helps me to get things right the next time around. The thing is, I'm not interested in making things right in some relationship down the road, because I know that whoever comes along won't hold a candle to you."

More oohs and ahs sounded. Samantha fanned her face with her notecards.

Camila, on the other hand, was welcoming the warmth in her blood. The pool of happiness floating around her heart. The word elation came to mind. And that's what it was, in its most tentative form, waiting to burst into a broader state of joy.

"I miss you. I love...everything about you. And I'm asking you to forgive me."

"Whoo-wee!" Samantha rested her hands on James' knee. "*I forgive you.*"

The crowd burst into laughter. Camila did too.

"Oh, you weren't talking to me, were you?" Samantha cooed. "Well, whoever this woman is, she's lucky. And if she doesn't hit you up after the show, I'll always be right here."

The camera started to pan out, and suddenly Camila remembered where she was and what she was doing. Quickly then, she wiped the happy tears from her cheeks, washed up at the sink once more, and got back to work preparing a meal she was now very excited to create. Boy, was her mind buzzing. And if Gypsy had seen what Camila just had, her phone would be buzzing soon too.

James' phone came alive in the aftermath of the show. Everyone from his PA to his sister to his mom. But the one James' responded to first—once he was settled into the backseat of the limo—was Duke's text.

Duke: *Way to put it all out there for a chick, man. Maybe this one is for keeps.*

James fought to wipe the grin off his face. There was no guarantee here, well he knew it. But he also had the undeniable feeling that he and Camila were written in the stars. *Please say she'll forgive me.*

He hurried and tapped out a reply.

James: *If I have it my way, it will definitely be for keeps.*

Duke: *Wait, this is the chick you "accidentally" asked to marry you once? I have a feeling you're going to be the first Benton married. That would be pretty wild, considering that you're the youngest.*

James: *You never know...*

He sent that last one with a smile on his face, one that faltered as he scrolled down the list of texts that had come in. Nothing from Camila yet. Which was fine; she was busy at work.

Still, a spark of fear flared in his gut. Perhaps this wouldn't result in the ending he hoped for. Sure, Camila was busy catering a party for Shane—the one who'd made sure she'd seen the interview, bless him. And sure, James didn't *actually* expect her to be the one to reach out. That was on him.

The appearance on the show had been the perfect way to let her know—before she slammed the door on his face or blocked his calls—that he was sorry. Now it was time to go one step further. He only hoped she'd be willing to hear him out.

CHAPTER 26

*C*amila whistled a love song as she hoisted her cooking supplies from the back seat of her car. With stacked crates balancing on her forearms, she used her hip to bump the car door closed.

The pale blue glow of twilight lit her way as she carted her supplies toward the wide steps in front of her apartment building. Crickets chirped from the surrounding hedges, their happy echo competing with the sounds of nearby traffic.

Heaven must have helped her get through tonight's catering job after seeing James' live interview. Several times throughout the evening, Camila had forced herself to rein in the excitement. After all, she wasn't even sure what would come of it.

James had said he was in love with her on live TV. *Wow!* And hadn't he also said he loved everything about her? And that he hoped she would forgive him?

In a way, she already had. Mainly because she understood

why he'd panicked over the submission. At least, the logical side of her did.

Camila had had to assure herself at least two dozen times that the interview had *really* happened. As dreamlike as it might have been, she hadn't imagined seeing James on TV. She'd seen him, she'd heard him, and she couldn't wait to see him face-to-face.

But how was she supposed to proceed from here? He'd gone so far as to speak about her during his interview—speak *to* her, actually. Hopefully he wouldn't stop there.

Just then, she heard something coming from the top of the stairs. A man clearing his throat. She peeked over the stack of boxes she carried and caught sight of a tall, dark, and seriously gorgeous man in a three-piece suit. The very suit he'd been wearing on live TV.

"James?" His name carried all the surprise she felt at the sight of him.

He cracked a wide grin. "Camila." It had been several days since she'd heard him say her name, in person anyway, that deep voice, complete with accent and all. She'd missed it.

Camila knew well that certain views could take her breath away, but seeing James standing in front of her place in all his suit-and-tie glory? That took her mobility too. It must have, because she'd stopped walking altogether.

"Hi," she squeaked.

James hurried down the steps and moved across the walkway with long, purposeful strides.

It was a good thing she had the crates to keep her arms occupied, because every fiber in her wanted to wrap them around James, pull him in for a long, satisfying embrace, and breathe in his heavenly smell.

"Can I help you get these inside?" He didn't wait for an answer. Instead, James positioned himself before her and slipped his arms under the crates alongside hers.

At once the weight was lifted, and James moved into place beside her. "What floor are you on? The top one?"

She liked that he remembered that; she'd mentioned it once. "Yes."

"I've been guessing that the one up there, with the blue and white hammock, is yours."

She grinned as she followed his gaze to the upper corner. "Was it really the hammock that gave me away, or all the potted herbs our neighbor had to water for us while Gypsy and I were gone?"

He grinned. "Both."

The conversation was put on pause as Camila led James to the elevator, down the brightly lit hall, and into her quiet apartment.

Her mind was a different story though. Suddenly, it started some sort of monologue. Rehearsing all types of terrible things James might say to her. She worked to get it under control. *Hope, Camila. Focus on hope.* Had she already forgotten his interview? That said it all, didn't it?

"Is right here good?" James asked.

Camila closed her apartment door and spun to see the crates hovered over her kitchen counter.

"Yes," she blurted. "That's perfect. Thank you."

James set them in place before stepping away from the counter. He glanced about the place for a bit, prompting a whole new monologue to run through her mind. Something like: *What kind of crappy place is this?*

A smile pulled at his lips. "It's nice in here," he said softly. "Your apartment…it looks like you." He strode to the side table and leaned down to study the picture she had framed. An image of Camila and her mother. Just a candid one Grandpa took at her fifth birthday party.

"Wow," he said with the shake of his head. "You look a lot alike. She's beautiful."

Camila nodded. "Thank you." A bout of nerves rushed through her as he stepped over to the bookcase next, eyeing the large selection of books.

"Let me guess, this side—with all the holistic type stuff is Gypsy's. And this…" He leaned closer to inspect the books on that side. "With all the culinary books and romance novels must be yours."

"Right." Camila had never come out and told James of her love for romance novels, but he'd caught her curled up with a few during their stay at the resort. "Should we sit?" Camila asked before he started wandering toward the bedrooms. The truth was, she was anxious to get this part—whatever it might entail—behind her.

"Sure." He strode across her living room in all his glory, looking out of place in the modest surrounding. Which raised yet another inward doubt about their fate as a couple.

He sank into the couch and gave the cushion beside him a pat.

A new knot of nerves kicked to life. "Should I make some tea?" she asked, suddenly desperate to put off the talk.

"In a minute." James gave the couch another pat. He

attempted a smile, she could tell that much, but the look in his eyes gave him away—James was anxious too.

A tight gulp slunk down her throat. "Okay."

She sat down beside him, her arm barely brushing against his, and caught scents of his heavenly cologne in an instant.

"I've missed you," James said.

Camila glanced over, caught that brooding look on his face, and felt her heart melt. "I've missed you too," she admitted. "So much."

She watched his face transform in response. The furrow along his brow softening as a full, glorious smile pulled at his lips.

Heaven help her.

"We have a lot to talk about," he said. "But most importantly, I want you to know that I'm so sorry. I was an idiot to think— even for a minute—that I couldn't trust you. I shouldn't have needed Gypsy to tell me—"

"So it *was* Gypsy? She's the reason you're here?" She'd known it was a possibility, but Camila had hoped that he'd... only she didn't know how to finish that sentence.

"Camila," James said. "I wish you would have told me when you found out. That explains everything, and I think I had a right to know."

"You're right." Camila nodded, gulped, and tried to shift the words from her head to her lips. "I think that...more than expecting or hoping for you to figure it out on your own, I was afraid that—even if you knew the truth—you wouldn't want me back. Like, maybe all of this was just an excuse to end things?" She'd ended it like a question, though she hadn't meant to.

It was just that, those thoughts were easy to believe when James was nowhere in sight. But saying them directly to him while looking into those deep blue eyes, that was a different story.

James shook his head as he answered. "No, never. I *want* you in my life, Camila." He leaned closer, brought a hand to the side of her neck, and held her gaze as if willing her to see the truth for herself. "I hope you believe that."

Tension drained from her shoulders as she let his declaration sink in.

James trailed his fingers down the back of her neck, softly, slowly. "*And* I hope that you'll forgive me for flipping out over the whole thing."

"I do," she was quick to say.

James froze suddenly. His eyes went wide. "You do? You forgive me?"

She grinned. "Of course."

Camila barely had time to finish the word when James pulled her in for a full embrace. "I've been so worried that I'd lost you forever."

"I was worried about that too." She ran her hand up the muscled contours of his upper back, relishing the feel of him in her arms.

"I love you, Camila," he said into the nook of her neck. His lips grazed her earlobe, causing a wave of chills to ripple over her skin.

"I love you, too," she said.

He moved in to kiss her cheek next, once, twice, before his full and glorious kiss was hers at last.

Camila cleared her mind of all else and focused on the

perfection of James' incredible kiss. Coaxing, alluring, heavenly. Impossibly better than she recalled.

"I've got one more thing to tell you," James said against her mouth.

Camila pressed another kiss to his lips. "Can it wait?"

He smiled. "It's good. I promise."

She watched as he tugged a folded magazine from his suit coat pocket. "Okay, first, I have to tell you that I found out about your parents. I'm guessing that's what you were going to tell me on that last day at the villa?"

Camila backed up in question, taken aback by the shift in topic. "Yeah."

"Listen," James said, "I was so sorry to learn about that. The fact that you had to deal with something so tragic, and no doubt confusing…"

She nodded tentatively.

"Well, I found out that your mother had something published. Did you know she liked to write?"

Camila shook her head. But then she nodded as she recalled something Grandma told her. "Yes, actually. She liked to write poems."

A wide smile crossed James' lips. "Yes. I think she had this published quietly, behind your father's back, perhaps. I'm guessing your grandmother hadn't known about it either, or else she would have told you."

A sudden urgency pricked at her from the inside.

"I know it's not as much as Winston left behind," he said, "but it's definitely something. And as you'll soon see, she wrote it with you in mind."

He handed over the magazine, a worn copy folded open to a

certain page, and wrapped his arm around her back as she hovered over it.

I Hope You'll Know
By Isabella Lakes

If I should leave the turning globe
before my time is through,
I hope you'll know the utter love
that I have for you.

I hope you'll remember the times we sang
to Bowie blasting loud.
The times I put you on my shoulders
when walking through a crowd.

I hope you'll have memories of my voice
saying I love you.
But in case you don't, then please hear this,
my sweet, sweet 'Mila, I do.

I don't plan to part, but if I do,
know that I won't be far.
In the sun and the breeze and the garden you grow,
I'll be wherever you are.

. . .

Camila hugged the magazine—the absolute treasure—to her chest as tears and sobs overcame her. She could never have expected to hear from her mom after all these years, yet here it was—a gift. Given to her by the man she'd given her heart to.

"How did you get this?" she managed through a jagged breath.

"I have my ways," he mumbled. "Once I found out she had something published, I put a team on the hunt. Discovered there was a copy at the old library downtown. It was there, in the back department, stacked in boxes." He chuckled. "But I assured the woman helping me it was for a very good cause."

Indeed it was. "Thank you."

James pressed a kiss to the top of her head. "You're welcome," he said with a sniff. "Your mom must be determined, like you. I'm guessing she's the one who made sure we found it."

Camila grinned, entertaining the idea for herself. "Yeah," she said with a nod. "I bet you're right."

It would take years to soak in the truth of it for herself—her mother really did love her. Enough to secretly leave a little something behind. It made her realize something else too. She turned to James, looked over his handsome face, and reveled in the peace and hope blooming in her heart.

"You know what else she wanted me to find?"

James tipped his head to one side. "What?"

"Well, with the help of my grandparents and *your* loved ones too," Camila added as more warmth filled her heart. "They wanted me to find *you*."

"Absolutely," James agreed through a laugh of his own. He came in for another kiss.

This time, Camila pulled him in even closer. She'd learned something in all of her years in the culinary field—it was important to slow down and savor the taste of every meal. Food took time to harvest, prepare, and present, but it was well worth the wait.

Love seemed to be that way too. It was no easy feat finding the right one, so when it finally happened, when one finally had him in her arms with his mouth on hers, it was best to savor each sensation. And now, Camila looked forward to tasting all that a life with James had to offer.

EPILOGUE

"*Y*ou nervous?" Duke hissed.

"Umm..." James sank a hand into his pocket and cupped the small, velvet box in his palm. His already speeding pulse revved hotter at the reminder of what he was about to do. "Yes. Of *course* I'm nervous. I just want it to go well, you know?" He tipped his head around the log-fashioned wall to see the happenings in the main floor of the cabin. It had been over six months since Camila had come to the life celebration gathering, where she met his family for the very first time.

Now, Betzy, Mom, and Camila were inseparable. He hadn't expected Camila's excitement for food to rub off on the two, but it had. Both Mom and Betzy had taken to preparing meals on a semi-regular basis.

Even now, as the three bustled around the kitchen, excited chatter and light laughter filled the cabin. Zander and Grandma

Lo, seated in the nearby living area, were caught up in conversation with Michael, Mom's new boyfriend.

James' gaze landed on Camila as she patted her hands on the apron she wore. *So beautiful.*

"I knew you were going to get married before the rest of us," Duke said. "Lucky dog."

The comment was enough to snap James from his musings. "Since when do *you* want to get married?"

Duke shrugged. "Since I've seen the way you guys worship the ground the other walks on. It's time someone did that for me."

James rolled his eyes. He knew Duke was kidding, about his reason for wanting to get married in the least. Most likely, he was joking about wanting to get married at all.

"So, when do you want to do this already?" Duke asked. "I have a feeling this is going to put the food on hold, and we can't let that happen for long. It smells too good."

Yes, it did smell good. But James wouldn't have his appetite back until he finished what he'd set out to do. "Soon," James answered. "Just waiting for Gypsy to come back in and give me the cue." He shifted his gaze to the back entry, where Camila's friend had snuck out to greet the florist.

Another bout of nervous energy fluttered through him. Suddenly, the distinct creak of the back screen door caught James' attention. Gypsy appeared in the clearing and shot James a thumbs up.

The sight was a fan to the flames within him. "Oh, man. It's time. Okay. You go down there with everyone, I'll sneak out from the patio. Gypsy might need help getting everyone out there, so…"

Duke nodded. "I'll help her." The grin that pulled at his brother's lips was a familiar one. And while it gave James pause, he couldn't exactly think on it right then.

He nodded. "Okay. Perfect." He nodded some more. "Thanks."

Duke gave him a smack on the arm. "Good luck, man." He surprised James by pulling him in for a hug then. "I'm proud of you," he said. "Seriously, you're my hero."

The comment had James recalling Winston's journal entry. The one that depicted him as a superhero, cape, gerbil sidekick, and all. James had shared those entries and sketches with his family at the celebration gathering, and boy, had they been a hit. Having waited a year to go through them hadn't seemed so bad after all. In a way, it was like hearing from Winston one last time.

James shifted his mind back to the matter at hand as he hurried back into the suite and onto the balcony. A set of wooden steps took him to ground level, where the flowers had, indeed, been placed to perfection.

It was beautiful. Just what Camila deserved for this special moment in her life. And hopefully, she'd recognize the gesture and know what James aimed to accomplish: representing the family who weren't able to be there. He stepped into place, tucked a hand into his pocket once more, and waited for the group to come. More than ever before, today felt like the first day of the rest of his life. The life he'd been meant to live all along.

Camila ran a quick gaze over the plates before her.

"Do they look right?" Betzy asked. "Because I don't think mine look as pretty as yours. What am I doing wrong?"

"I think mine look just right," Claudia said. She nudged Camila. "Don't you agree?"

Camila grinned. "Yes. And Betzy, the only thing missing from your plates is the garnish. See?"

"I *knew* there was something." Betzy snatched a few sprigs of rosemary from the bunch and tucked each beside the crusted bread on the meals she'd plated. "There. I love this job. I think I would *love* your job, Camila. At least, I like making things look pretty. And I like eating too."

"Who doesn't?" Gypsy asked, stepping back into the kitchen.

"Where'd you run off to?" Camila asked.

"Oh, nowhere. Actually, I was out front, and I saw a couple of deer out there. Do you guys want to see?"

Camila ran her hands under the sink. "They're out front?"

"Yeah," Gypsy said with a nod. "Come on."

"Okay," Camila agreed. She'd been charmed by the wildlife they'd seen at the cabin since the first time she'd come. Squirrels, chipmunks, moose, and deer.

"I think I'll get started on the wine," Claudia said as she strode over to the counter.

"Actually, Mom..." Duke said, coming up behind her. He exchanged a look with Gypsy. "I want you to try out the new rocking chair I had delivered."

The group shuffled toward the front door, Gypsy skipping as she led the way. And while that was a very Gypsy thing to do, Camila got the impression that something was up. Which reminded her...

"Hey, where's James?" Earlier, James and Duke had gone out to chop firewood. Camila loved that with all the money they had, and all the help they could hire, the Benton brothers still did manly things like chop wood on their own. At least out here at the family cabin.

But if Duke was back, then James should be too.

The sudden still that came over the crowd changed the tone in a blink. Camila heard at least two other gasps before one pulled from her own throat. The area surrounding the cabin had been transformed. As it was, towering redwoods, spruces, and firs surrounded the massive cabin in Big Bear Lake. A river flowed nearby, bringing a scattering of wildlife through the area.

But now there was a new addition. Camellia flowers— everywhere. Pots, plant holders, and vases lined the walkway. Some in copper, others in glass. Some even bloomed from wood-slatted buckets. The gorgeous blossoms were clustered by color. The ivory blooms stood taller along the back, the pale pink flowers dotted each corner. From there, as the clusters and rows led right up to the front porch, the hues shifted to shades of subtle pink to a deep, beautiful rouge.

Hundreds of petals dotted the clearing as well, creating a giant heart shape. Camila felt like her limbs were turning into goo. Was this the moment she thought it was?

"Would you take a look at that," Grandma Lo bellowed. She stood next to Zander, a hand tucked at the nook of his arm as she gazed at the clearing.

And that's when James appeared. He'd been hiding out beneath the foliage, she realized, as he strode onto the paved path, hands behind his back.

Betzy and Claudia huddled together, whispering as Camila made her way to the steps. Gypsy and Duke mumbled something as well.

James met her at the stairs and extended an arm, steadying her as she took the few, short steps down to him. He brought her to the center of the heart, dropped to one knee, and looked up in her eyes.

"Camila," James started, securing her other hand in his.

Goosebumps rushed over her skin as she locked eyes with him. Those blue depths she'd come to know and love so much.

"The last few months of my life have been the best I've ever had. I've loved discovering the beautiful woman you are. I fell in love with you, your passion, and your contagious zest for life."

The excitement stirring within her made her breaths come short and fast. But as James squeezed her hand and gave her a playful wink, she pulled in a deeper, longer breath. Her shoulders loosened too.

"We've talked about building a life together. Having a family together. And being there for each other through all the good and the bad."

She nodded as tears pierced her eyes. *Yes, they had.* And she could hardly believe this moment had finally come. Making it all the sweeter was the fact that James knew the dark, once-secret pieces of her past. He was proposing marriage to the true her, dark past and all.

He tucked a hand into his pocket, produced a small, velvet box, and flicked it open, revealing a gorgeous diamond ring. "Camila Lopez, would you do me the tremendous honor of being my wife?"

She was floating, Camila was sure of it. The deep burst of hope lifted her feet right off the ground. She wiped back tears as she nodded. "Yes," she said, sniffing. "Of course!"

An explosion of cheers erupted from the small crowd as James wrapped his arms solidly around her. She basked in the peaceful warmth of his embrace, the heavenly scent of his favorite aftershave, and comfort of his strength as he swept her off her feet and spun in place. He kissed her then, while a round of oohs and ahs echoed into the trees.

It turned out she wasn't the only one nervous. James' hand was trembling along with hers as he slid the ring onto her finger. "Can't wait to do that on our wedding day," he said under his breath before kissing her once more.

"I got all that recorded," Gypsy said from behind, "so that means I get to congratulate you guys first, right?"

Camila couldn't help but squeal as Gypsy pulled her in for an exuberant hug. "I'm so happy for you," she squealed in return.

Betzy, Claudia, and Michael were next in line to congratulate them, followed by Zander, and eventually Duke. "Guess you two are really tying the knot, huh? Goodbye, bachelorhood," he said while slapping a hand on James' shoulder.

James set his eyes on Camila. "Goodbye, bachelorhood and hello, beautiful wife." He tugged Camila's hand and pulled her in for another kiss.

"That's enough of that," Duke said. "No, but really. I'm sure you guys will actually *enjoy* married life. To each his own, right, Gypsy?"

Gypsy shot Duke a look. "To each *her* own."

Duke lifted a brow. "Hmm, sassy."

"It's about time one of my grandkids gets married," Grandma Lo grumbled as she pushed through the crowd. "Does an old lady have to live forever in order to see it for herself? Now let me hug my future granddaughter."

The woman tossed her arms around Camila, squished her tight, then pulled back to square a look at her with those pale blue eyes. "Welcome to the family, dear."

A deep feeling of peace settled over her. *Family.* She'd be part of a family again. The joy that knowledge gave her filled every fiber. Swelled until it lifted her very soul. "Thank you," she said, warmth swirling around her heart. "I'm excited to be a part of it."

Grandma Lo shielded her mouth with the back of her hand. "Now we've just got to get the rest of them married before I kick the bucket."

Camila laughed as the woman shuffled back toward the covered porch.

With James still huddled in conversation, Camila took a moment to enjoy the beautiful flowers, and the soft beams of sunlight piercing their way through the thick, leafy trees. She lifted her chin slightly, and a light breeze tickled her forehead.

Suddenly a vision rushed to her mind—of her mother brushing hair from her face with the soft tips of her fingers. Lovingly, softly, her brown eyes wide and kind.

Camila hadn't recalled such a moment before, but now it was clear as day. And as it played through her mind once more in perfect clarity, she realized that it was a recollection, indeed. One gifted to her in the breeze.

She took in the beautiful camellia flowers, appreciating the way James had used them in honor of the family no longer with her. She was grateful for it, and hopeful that, somehow, their loved ones were witnessing this special moment. Cheering from somewhere beyond the clouds.

"I've got one more little thing over here," James said, coming up beside her.

Camila looped a hand through his arm and rested her head on his shoulder as they walked. He led her through a windy, overgrown path, the way thick with dusty leaves, dry pine needles, and the wonderful scents of the forest.

He slowed at a tree with a list of letters carved into it. At first, it appeared rather random, but a closer look said each carving served a purpose. At the top, a heart outlined a pair of initials. C.O—for Claudia Osworth, she guessed, and JB for Jonathon Benton. A tiny plus sign joined the set together.

Below that, came the initials DB, ZB, BB, JB, and at last, WB. "These are for each of us, kids. Winston, of course, carved a little something next to his."

Camila tilted her head to see the tiny words *the coolest one* scratched into the wood next to Winston's initials. She couldn't help but laugh.

"We've told my mom that, if she and Michael get married, she can carve a new heart into the tree. Beneath all the kids, since that marks the order of things." He motioned to the area beyond the tree.

"Those two over there, you may have already noticed them, they have my grandparents initials carved into them. Both my mom and Dad's sides, and their kids too. But here...here's where ours is."

Leaves crunched beneath her shoes as Camila approached the tall, bark-covered trunk. She lifted a hand, traced the tip of her finger over the carved lines, imagining a time, long ago, when James' very own dad lovingly scratched the letters into the wood. "This is awesome," she breathed. "Your family tree. I love it."

James nestled into her cheek, sighed, then planted a kiss to her skin. "What do you say we start one of our own?"

Camila lifted a brow and turned to him. "You happen to have a knife on you?" She hadn't yet gotten over the fluttery feel in her tummy when she looked at his handsome face.

"As a matter of fact...I do." James pulled a small pocketknife from his suit coat. "Pick a neighboring tree, any one you'd like, and it'll be ours."

Camila grinned, pulling in a deep breath as she lifted her gaze to the trees. A memory of James looking over the novels on her bookshelf came to mind. Each one of her favorite stories was wrapped up with a happy ending—like a lovely package with a pretty bow.

And as she eyed the surrounding trees, looking for just the right one, she mused that—in the literary world—this might be where her own happily ever after ended the book. But of course, this was really only the beginning. As years would pass, Zander, Betzy, and maybe even Duke would carve hearts into a tree of their own with that special someone.

God willing, they'd each get to add a few letters below that heart as their families grew. She could picture the little ones now, dashing through the trees in a game of tag. Building snowmen on a winter's day, only to rush onto the large porch, unload heavy boots, colorful scarfs, and mismatched mittens before running inside.

They'd warm their fingers at the fireplace while retelling

their wintery tales and, perhaps, be interested in hearing a few tales in return. Of the time their folks fell in love, and how their very own story began.

Camila sighed, realizing now, more than ever, that despite the difficulties life's journey often lent, the heavens had a way of making things right again. Life went on, indeed, and it was her job to make the very most of it. She grinned as just the right tree caught her eye, inwardly promising to do just that.

The End

SAMPLE CHAPTER

$\mathcal{T}$hank you for reading 28 Days With A Billionaire. Want more from the Benton Brothers Series? Read a sample from Book 2, Her Best Friend Fake Fiancé, below.

Her Best Friend Fake Fiancé
   by Kimberly Krey

"You're not going to believe what Kellianne just brought me."

Betzy's heart pumped a clumsy beat out of rhythm. Kellianne, as in Sawyer Kingsley's mom. She and her mom had been close since Kellianne started cleaning house for their family years ago. "What was it?"

Mom dug into her bag, pulled out a magazine, and plopped it on the center of the table next to the decorative butterballs and bread bowl.

Betzy's eyes shot to the headline:

Most Eligible Bachelors From East Coast to West.

"Again?" Betzy was the first one to snatch the magazine off the table and pull it to her chest.

"This one's with *Slipper Magazine,*" Mom said. "Last time it was *World's Way.*"

Quickly, Betzy flipped page after page, not bothering to look at the index in front.

Advertisement.

Another advertisement.

Portland's Bachelor.

Makeup tips.

Washington's…Tampa's…

Him. Sawyer Kingsley, one of New York City's top real estate moguls, right there in black and white. And what a stunning picture it was.

Betzy steadied her breath; it felt like a jackhammer was going off inside her chest. The photographer had opted for the night-after-a-long-day look. His white, button-up shirt hung open, revealing a generous view of his sculpted pecs and chiseled abs. The ends of a skinny black tie dangled at either side. In the photo on the left, Sawyer looked off in the distance, his squared jaw and furrowed brow giving him a pensive expression.

She knew that expression well. Loved it.

"I can't believe he didn't tell me about this," Betzy mumbled.

"Maybe he's humble," Camila said over her shoulder.

Rachel hovered over the other side. "No one *that* good looking knows humility."

Betzy grinned, partly amused by their dialogue, and partly

wistful as she recalled the walking contradiction of Sawyer Kingsley. He played a cocky male as well as the next guy, with his flirtatious ways and bold, charismatic smile, but beneath that, there was a humble quality. An endearing one at that.

Her eyes drifted to the photo on the right. He was looking straight into the lens in that one, running a hand through his hair with a smile that made her heart quiver and ache.

She'd earned a whole lot of those smiles over the years, but that thought only added to the hurt.

How? How after all this time was she not over Sawyer? She'd sent a piece of her heart with him when he left to New York, secretly hoping he'd come back and marry her. But as the years passed, Betzy realized he'd never promised any such thing.

She gulped past a shallow breath, cursing the heated longing deep in her chest. It reminded her of the incident she tried very hard to forget. The one that forced Betzy to snatch that part of her heart back and bury it. Bury it deep like a worm in the ground.

But all too often, her mind became the beak of a bird, piercing through the soil to snatch it up and devour it whole.

Not right now, Betzy. Don't revisit that right now. She wouldn't. What she *would* do is send Mr. hot, sexy bachelor of NYC a text. Just to prove she could. How many women ogling his spread could do that? Not many, ladies. Not many.

She pulled her phone from her purse and tapped out a text to the one and only.

Betzy: *Check out our lunch conversation topic at the clubhouse today.*

She snapped a picture of his magazine spread and hit send.

"Who's that going to?" Camila asked.

Betzy glanced up from her phone to see that Grandma, Rachel, and Mom awaited her answer as well. "It's to him."

Camila gripped hold of her forearm. "You really do *know* this guy?"

Betzy grinned. Her new sister-in-law was the only one at the table who didn't know about their history.

Rachel pulled out the finger quotes. "They're *friends.*"

A grin spread over Camila's face. "Have you ever kissed him?" That question, sweetened by her Spanish accent, rolled off Camila's tongue with far too much ease.

"Camila," Betzy said with a gasp.

"Well," Grandma Lo blurted. *"Have* you?"

Betzy made a quick survey of the table before nodding ever so slightly.

The ladies' chorus of oohs and ahs gained attention from nearby patrons. It was a good thing Rachel wasn't still shooting pictures of her since Betzy was likely red all the way to her toes.

"Hello, lovely ladies," their table host said cheerily. "Have you made your selections yet?"

Slowly, hesitantly, the eyes peeled away from Betzy and shifted to their host. And while they placed the ladies orders one by one, Betzy was replaying that heavenly kiss.

"Mind if I take a little peek at this for myself?" Rachel asked, gripping the corner with her finger and thumb.

Betzy shook her head. "No, go ahead." She watched numbly as Rachel licked a finger and turned the page.

"Maybe I'll snatch up one of these other bachelors for myself," Rachel said under her breath.

"What magazine is that?" Camila asked.

"*Slipper*," Mom answered. "Hey, that reminds me. Don't the Shays run *Slipper Magazine?*"

Betzy resisted an eye-roll. "Yep."

"That's what I thought. Kellianne says the editor went to school with you and Sawyer. What's her name?"

"Daisy," Betzy said. "*Daisy Shay...*" She added emphasis to help Mom recognize the name. Daisy had caused Betzy a whole lot of grief during their school years. Spreading false rumors and going after any guy Betzy took an interest in, namely Sawyer.

"That's right," Mom said as enlightenment lit her eyes. "I guess Daisy personally delivered three copies of the magazine to Kellianne the day the issue came out."

"I bet she did," Betzy said under her breath. Irritation gripped her fast and hard. Seemed as if Daisy still wanted to get her hands on Sawyer. At one point, she'd accomplished that very thing. Was she simply up to her same old tricks?

Betzy's phone buzzed with a reply just as the host made his way to her. Quickly, she ordered the brie cheese wedge with tomato bisque and handed over the menu. A smile crossed her lips as she saw the name on the screen.

Sawyer: *Me, your lunchtime topic? You don't say. I'm flattered.*

Betzy: *Don't be. Half of the party's over the age of fifty.*

Sawyer: *All the more flattering.*

Betzy: *I guess you're right. Have fun sleeping at night knowing that old women find you sexy.*

Sawyer: *I will. But the more important question is this: do YOU find me sexy?*

Heat flared hot in her chest, neck, and face.

"Did he text you back?" Camila asked.

"Yeah," Betzy said. "Here." She tipped the phone so Camila could read the interaction herself.

"He's a flirt," she said with a grin.

"I know." Another text popped up.

Sawyer: *Is that crickets I hear chirping? C'mon, is it that hard to admit you're attracted to me?*

Betzy shook her head. "Incorrigible." It took her a moment to think of a response, but at last, it came to her.

Betzy: *I can admit that all sorts of men are sexy. It doesn't mean they're my type.*

Sawyer: *Women. Always so complicated.*

A deep, happy sigh spilled through her lips as she looked at the screen. She enjoyed this. Would miss it once it was gone. Which it would be once Sawyer got serious with someone. It was probably the only way she'd really know he'd gotten into a relationship.

"Hey, look what's coming in next month's issue," Rachel said, pointing at a spot on the back page. Betzy read it aloud as she went.

"From hard-working bachelorette to wealthy old spinster. Find out which billionaire bachelorettes are destined to hold onto their money while *men* slip through their fingers."

A hush fell over the table.

A sick knot formed in Betzy's stomach as she reread the title. "You are *kidding* me."

She snatched the magazine from Rachel to see it up close and personal. "I bet you anything I'm on that list."

"You're in your twenties," Grandma countered, but that crease along her brow said she was concerned just the same.

"It doesn't say she's *already* a spinster," her mom said, "just that she's destined to *become* one."

Grandma and Mom exchanged a worried glance.

"Who else do we know that works for *Slipper?*" Mom asked. "We need to know if she's on that list."

Betzy turned her eyes on Grandma next. "Anyone? Think."

Grandma gritted her teeth and snatched her phone from her purse. "I'll ask around. Don't you worry, dear. I doubt they would ever put you on a list like that."

Mom locked eyes with Betzy across the table, her lips pursed in concentration. After all of Mom's warnings that Betzy might end up alone if she pursued a career, there wasn't a hint of *I-told-you-so* in her gaze.

Claudia Benton knew how to play that mama bear role as well as the rest of them, especially when it was to protect the family name.

Betzy imagined the humiliation that might come of it—an appearance in an article that said she was destined to be old and all alone. The very fear that had haunted Betzy since she was a little girl.

Grandma and all of her gumption had given her the courage to compete in the business world with the best of the best and make a name for herself, despite her mother's warning.

The trouble was, that warning might just hold true. A knot of burning heat stirred in her gut.

She would definitely be on that list. And she could guess at who's idea it'd been to put her there: Daisy Shay's.

Camila gave her a tap on the arm and leaned in. "Hey, James is heading out of town with Zander later today. Why don't you come over? We'll come up with a plan to combat the article just in case, and you can fill me in on your history with this sexy bachelor. Oh, and of course, we'll eat something amazing."

Camila wasn't just saying that either. As one of LA's finest private chefs, James' new wife turned ordinary meals into something of magic.

"Rachel can come too, if you'd like," she added.

Betzy gave Camila a grin, grateful to finally have a sister at last. "Thank you," she said. "I'd love that." She glanced down at her phone to see if Sawyer had texted anything more. He hadn't, which left his latest words like black dots against the white screen. *Women. Always so complicated.*

But she had to disagree. Sawyer Kingsley—*he* was the complicated one. No matter how many times Betzy had hoped something might happen between them, she'd met with one too many disappointments in that regard.

He was, in a way, untouchable. Sadly, she would likely never kiss those lips again. Unless, Betzy mused wryly, she wanted to kiss the pages of that magazine.

This ends the sample of Her Best Friend Fake Fiancé.

FREE BOOK

Subscribe to my newsletter and receive my novella, Ranch Hand for Auction, FREE as a thank you gift!

ALSO BY KIMBERLY KREY

Billionaires In Hiding Romance Series

Springtime Love at The Homestead Inn: Country Boy & City Girl

Summer Nights at The Homestead Inn: While He Was Sleeping

Autumn Romance at The Homestead Inn: Do Nice Guys Finish Last?

Winter Kisses at The Homestead Inn: Flirting With the Enemy

Cabin Fever at The Homestead Inn: Despite the Odds

The Sweet Montana Bride Series

Reese's Cowboy Kiss

Jade's Cowboy Crush

Cassie's Cowboy Crave

Taja's Cowboy Caress

More Cowboy Romance:

The Cowboy's Catch

Unlikely Cowgirl Series

Her Gun-shy Cowboy

Her Kismet Cowboy

Her Dream Cowboy

Small Town Romance:

Cobble Creek Small Town Romance

The Unlikely Bride

The Hopeful Bride

The Determined Bride

Second Chances Series

Rough Edges

Mending Hearts

Fresh Starts

Benton Brothers Romance

28 days with a Billionaire

Her Best Friend Fake Fiancé

Stepping In For The Billionaire Groom

The Billionaire's Second Chance

The Billionaire's (Not So) Fake Engagement

Romantic Comedies

Five Days With My Super Hot Ex

Five Days With My Kinda Evil Ex

Six Days With My Celebrity Ex

My Grumpy Christmas Companion

Getting Kole for Christmas

Getting Micah under the Mistletoe

Beach Romance

Catching Waves: A Sweet Beach Romance (The Royal Palm Resort Book 2)

28 days with a Billionaire

Young Adult Novellas

Getting Kole for Christmas

Getting Micah under the Mistletoe

Chemistry of a Kiss

Novella

Ranch Hand for Auction

The Cowboy's Catch

Navy SEALs Romance

The Honorable Warrior

The Fearless Warrior

Christmas Romance

Her TV Bachelor Fake Fiancé

Her Best Friend Fake Fiancé

The Billionaire's (Not So) Fake Engagement

Snowed In For Christmas

Getting Kole for Christmas

Getting Micah under the Mistletoe

Dashing Through the Tropes

Collections

All's Fair in Love & Tropes

Benton Brothers Billionaire Romance Collection

ABOUT THE AUTHOR

Writing Romance That's Clean Without Losing the Steam!

Award-winning author Kimberly Krey has always been a fan of good, clean romance, so she decided to specialize in writing 'Romance That's Clean without Losing the Steam'. She's a fervent lover of God, family, and cheese platters, as well as the ultimate hater of laundry. Follow her on any of the sites below for updates on new releases and or giveaways.

facebook.com/kimberlykreyauthor
twitter.com/KimberlyKrey
instagram.com/romance_is_write
amazon.com/Kimberly-Krey/e/B009A0350I
bookbub.com/profile/kimberly-krey

ACKNOWLEDGEMENTS

Acknowledgements: (Recipe inspirations found here:)
https://spanishsabores.com/2012/06/12/recipe-carrillada-braised-iberian-pork-cheek-with-port-wine-and-honey/

Made in the USA
Monee, IL
07 August 2023

40568958R00157